D0555691

MEG EASTON

Clean romances with
fun-loving, unforgettable characters

Book Three in the Nestled Hollow Romance series

Cover Illustration by Covers and Cupcakes

Interior Design by Mountain Heights Publishing

Author website: www.megeaston.com

christmas at the end of main street

christmas at the end of main street

A NESTLED HOLLOW ROMANCE

MEG EASTON

MOUNTAIN HEIGHTS
— PUBLISHING —

contents

one

MACIE

Macie was sitting in the middle of her bedroom floor, putting on one of her running shoes, when her black lab pushed his way right into her space. "Reese! I can't reach my shoelaces!" The dog nuzzled his face into her neck, his feet scrambling to sit on her lap. Sometimes it seemed like he didn't even realize he wasn't a puppy. Macie gave up trying to tie her shoes and rubbed her fingers behind his ears and under his collar, just as he liked.

It wasn't long, though, before his scrambling legs knocked her right over, and Lola, her cream-colored Goldendoodle, joined Reese in licking her face. "Lola! Reese! I appreciate all the love, I do. But you both want to go for a run, right?" She pushed her way back to sitting, wove her arms through the jumble of dog legs, and managed to get both hands working to tie her shoelaces. Then she led the two big dogs out of the room she rented from her sister and brother-in-law, and into the open kitchen, dining room, and family room that she shared with them.

"Good morning," Macie said to Joselyn as her sister packed lunches for her family. Then she turned to her littlest niece, Aria, who sat in her high chair, and gave her a kiss on the cheek. Lola and Reese played their favorite game with Aria while Macie got their breakfast ready— taking turns hopping up in the air in front of Aria's high chair while Aria squealed with delight, occasionally throwing some of her food in their direction in her excitement.

"So," Joselyn said, drawing out the word, "how was your date last night?"

Macie's shoulders slumped at the memory.

"Oh, that good, huh?"

Macie put Reese's and Lola's dishes on the floor, and they raced to them, scarfing down their food. "It was fine. He was fine." She paused a moment, then added, "For someone else."

Joselyn's lips lifted into a smile. "I sense a story."

"He's just really, *really* loud. And strong. Which would've been great if I hadn't found that out because of his exuberance in playing 'Slug Bug.'" They had driven to Denver to go to a concert, and with more than two hours on the road, there had been a surprising number of Volkswagen Beetles along the way.

Joselyn winced. "Besides the 'slugging,' how was the drive? Any good conversation?"

"We didn't exactly find a conversation topic that interested both of us." She grabbed an apple out of the basket and washed it in the sink. "I have no idea why in the world Sherry thought we had so much in common when she set us up. Unless she meant that I am twenty-seven and not married and he is twenty-eight and not married. Because that's the only commonality we discovered."

Macie stood at the patio doors, looking out as the pre-dawn light just began to show the backyards that she and her siblings shared as she ate her apple. There were seven of them, and their parents had bought an entire square block of property in Nestled Hollow. Until her early teenage years, the property had been a big field they'd played in for hours each day.

Then, one by one as her siblings got married, each couple built a house for their new family on their own lot. Now her parents' house was at the top center of the square, her two older brothers' houses were on their left and right on the corners, her twin brothers finishing off the left side, Joselyn and Marcus had the bottom center, and her sister Nicole at the bottom right. All their backyards came together into one giant playground with picnic benches and fire pits and barbecues and shade trees, where all of her nieces and nephews played and they got together for family dinners every week.

Joselyn started cleaning off Aria's face with a wet cloth. "Don't worry. You'll find your Mr. Perfectly Right, I know it."

"Nope. I give up." She gestured at the one lot that remained empty— the lot that was hers that currently only held weeds and a single scraggly-looking tree that was shorter than her. "I'm just going to build a one-bedroom house there, buy a spinning wheel, maybe bring home a few cats from work."

Joselyn chuckled and was joined by Marcus's booming laugh as he entered the room. Macie joined in, Aria bounced in her seat, and the dogs ran in circles around them.

"I take it last night's date didn't go well?" Marcus asked. "My brother says he's got a friend who would be perfect—"

"No," Macie said, cutting him off. "No more blind dates."

"But—"

"No." Macie's voice came out more forceful than she meant, so she searched for the right words to explain. "I'm tired of having hope. Tired of hoping that a blind date will work out. And when it does work out, I'm tired of hoping that it'll turn into something more."

"So you're just going to stop dating?" Joselyn asked.

Macie nodded. "For six months." She hadn't made that decision until the words were out of her mouth. "I'm just going to focus on my business, and forget trying to find a future spouse."

"You know what Dad's going to say about that," Joselyn said as she lifted Aria out of her highchair.

Of course, she did. She'd heard him say often enough that her future spouse was a needle in a haystack, and that she had to be willing to search through a lot of hay to find him. She was even hearing it right now in her head, with his exact tone of voice and inflection.

"But here's what I figured out last night in between 'Slug bugs.' What if my needle isn't even in the haystack I'm searching in? What if my needle is in Myanmar or Denmark or Zimbabwe or wherever, and I never go there in my lifetime? What if I keep searching through my haystack and get through every single piece of hay, only to find that there was never a needle for me? That my perfect guy just isn't out there? I think I'll just tell Dad that for six months, I'm just going to let the wind clear away some of that hay for me."

"Even if you convince him," Marcus said, "your mom won't stop finding people with 'son-in-law qualities' to line you up with."

"People in town won't stop, either," Joselyn added, Aria bouncing on her hip.

Macie's breath came out in a sigh. She knew people lined her up with dates out of care, concern, and love, but they still felt like a force of nature that couldn't be stopped.

Lola came running up to Macie, her leash in her mouth, and seconds later, Reese joined her, also holding his leash. "Looks like it's time for me to head to work. Are you still free to chat business this afternoon?" She stretched out her calves, then bent down to attach their leashes.

Joselyn handed Aria off to Marcus. "Yep! Can you come to With a Cherry on Top at 4:30? We're usually pretty slow about that time."

"That'll work."

"Have you gotten any closer to deciding whether or not to buy your building?" Marcus asked.

The question itself made her chest tighten and her stomach churn. It was a weight on her shoulders all the time, even when she wasn't actively thinking about it. But she needed to be actively thinking about it more often. She'd been working toward opening Paws and Relax ever since she'd planned the business in her high school entrepreneur class. She knew she wanted to rescue animals from the county shelter that were desperate to be loved and have them available for people who were desperate to love an animal but couldn't have a pet in their home.

Even after thinking about it and planning it for years,

it still took a huge leap of faith to sign the lease on the building, and it renewed every six months. But the owner wanted to put the building up for sale on January first unless she let him know first that she wanted to buy it.

And buying it was so much more than a six-month commitment. If leasing the building was taking a leap of faith over a ditch, buying it was taking a leap of faith over a chasm so wide that she couldn't see the other side.

Macie put on her coat, gloves, scarf, and hat as she spoke. "Not yet. I've got four weeks from today to decide, so I'm going to try some new directions with my business, and see if I can make enough per month for it to work." It was going to be tough, and she wasn't sure she could do it. She picked up the leashes, and as the dogs pulled her to the door, she called out, "Looks like we're going then. See you all at four-thirty!"

Once outside, she said to Lola and Reese, "What do you think? Mountain trail or lake trail today?" As usual, Lola was the first to choose the direction. Always Lola. "Mountains, then."

She started with a slow jog, trying to get her muscles warmed up in such cold temperatures. At least it hadn't started snowing yet— snow made their morning run so much more difficult to pull off. Lola and Reese ran right alongside her as she jogged through the last few streets of homes. When she reached the area where the gradual slope of the valley turned into the steep climb of the mountainside, they turned right onto the dirt pathway.

The leaves had long since fallen and given way to the calm, crisp, clear winter air. The scene from here was different now, but every bit as beautiful. Without leaf-covered trees blocking her view, she could see the whole town from this vantage point, the sun that was just peeking over the mountain making the lake sparkle like spilled glitter.

Her home was the perfect distance from work— just over two miles. Long enough to get good exercise for her and the dogs, but short enough that she didn't show up to Paws and Relax all sweaty. Even in these temperatures, there were still quite a few people using the mountain trail. Every time she would pass by someone, Lola would run forward until the leash stopped her. "What's up today, girl? You're extra excited, aren't you?" Macie hoped she'd have a busy day at the shop to help give Lola the attention she needed.

Just ahead, a man on a bike was coming from town up to the trail. As he turned from the road onto the path, heading in her direction, Lola raced forward like she was shot out of a cannon, yanking the leash right out of Macie's hand. "Lola!" she yelled as the dog sprinted forward. "Come back here!"

But it was too late. Lola had run straight for the biker, causing him to swerve. As he swerved and she pivoted, her leash got caught up in his tire, and the man and his bike jerked to the side and crashed to the ground in a tangled mess of bike and man. Macie raced to his side and bent down to see if he was okay, but he was already struggling to get his leg out from under the bike. He limped to a standing position.

"Are you okay? I am so sorry!"

"I'm fine."

Except he was still not putting pressure down on his left leg. He shook it a few times like he was trying to shake off the pain or injury. Lola just stood by both of them, looking up and panting, like she was going to get scratched behind her ears for doing a good job. The man — a good-looking, lean man who was probably around Macie's age— started brushing the dirt off his clothes. Macie reached out and brushed some of the dirt off his shoulders and back, apologizing for Lola and for not holding the leash tightly enough.

"It's okay. Really." He bent down and grabbed his bike, pulling it upright. "I'll be just fine. If I don't hurry, though, I'll be late for work and it'll be a zoo, and then you never know what's going to turn up on your white board." He got back on his bike, and as he pedaled, his right leg doing the bulk of the work, he called over his shoulder, "Nice meeting you!"

Macie watched as the man cycled away, and felt bad that she hadn't done a single thing to help. This crash was a perfect metaphor for her relationships lately. They always crashed and burned. She turned her back on the man— and turned her metaphorical back on relationships — and faced the Goldendoodle in front of her. "Lola! We don't run ahead and cause bikers to crash!"

Lola at least had the decency to drop her head the tiniest fraction in remorse, before she stood on all fours right next to Reese, mirroring his perfect angel pose. Macie was still upset at Lola for her behavior, but then Lola looked back at her with those big brown eyes, her fur framing them in a look of innocent anticipation, and she couldn't stay mad. "Okay, we'll keep going, but you stay right here next to me. No running off."

The rest of the run went as expected. When they reached Main Street, Macie slowed to a walk to get her heart rate down, and they made their way down to the end of the street where her business, Paws and Relax, was just a small fenced-in yard away from her sister's and brother-in-law's ice cream shop.

She unlocked the door to Paws and Relax, let Lola and Reese off their leashes to play, and filled up the smaller dogs' dishes before going into the dog room. "Good morning, Piper, Cookie, and Zeus!" She let the little dogs out of their kennels and through the side door to the small yard to relieve themselves. It was one of the reasons why this building had been the perfect choice—it was the only one on all of Main Street that seemed to be made for dogs.

When they'd all done their business and came bounding back inside, she sat on the floor and let them climb all over her as she laughed and tried to pet them equally. "One day," she told them, "I'll have my own house and I will take you all home with me every single day. Hopefully, I'll have a husband and kids for you to climb all over, too." Then they all raced into the main room to get their breakfast and to play with Lola and Reese, while she went into the back room to get food for the cats.

She carefully carried their dishes and opened the door to the cat paradise room. Shadow was lounging under a platform, Sam was clawing at a post, and Jinx was sitting at the highest spot on the climbing toy. They all raced to her as she sat down the food. "Come on out whenever you want," she told them as she left, leaving their door open.

After feeding the fish, the hamsters, and the geckos, she flipped the sign on the front door to *Open*, and then turned to look at her big family of animals. Just being around them was already making her less stressed. Seeing customers who couldn't have their own pets for a variety of reasons come in and hang out with these guys was the icing on top of a pretty fantastic cake. It felt good to turn her back on dating completely and focus on her business. She didn't need to go looking for love. She had all the love she needed right here.

two

AARON

As soon as the discussion in the faculty lunchroom at Nestled Hollow High turned to dating, Aaron made a show of noticing the time and excusing himself. His group of friends already gave him enough grief about it— he didn't need any more.

The bell was seconds from ringing, and if it weren't for the topic change, he very well could have kept socializing and been late to class. He stopped by the copy room and picked up his stack, then hurried toward his classroom as quickly as he could while the hallways emptied. His left leg still hurt a bit, but at least he wasn't limping. His cell phone buzzed in his pocket, and he pulled it out and glanced at the text on his screen.

"Speak of the devils," he said to no one in particular and slid the message open. In a group text with his friends, Matt mentioned their weekly Wednesday night get-together. Then he texted, *Can you find your own date, Aaron? Or should we find one for you?*

Aaron shifted the stack of papers he was holding so he could type in a return text.

> Aaron: Afraid I'll win every game again if I don't have a date to distract me?

The bell rang when he was still four classrooms away. As soon as he stepped into his room, the talking died down to complete silence, all eyes on him. Aaron eyed them. "Good afternoon." He paused for a moment, trying to see if he could tell why they were acting weird. "What's up, guys?"

"Nothing," Allen said.

"Nothing at all," Kyle added.

Morgan rolled her eyes. "You guys are so smooth. We were just speculating about why you were late, Mr. Hall. That's all. So how are you doing? How was your Monday evening?"

"You guys first," Aaron said. "I haven't seen you since class on Friday. How was everyone's weekend?" This AP History class was his favorite to teach. At just eleven students, it was by far his smallest class. The kids were all bright, and they gelled in a way that classes rarely did. It made for some interesting and enlightening discussions on history.

Several of his students told about what they'd done over the weekend or on Monday, they all riffed back and forth on each other's comments, and class settled into something more normal.

Then one of the students, Alecia, asked to use his cell phone. He nearly pulled it out of his pocket— something he'd have never done with any of his other classes, but then he realized that everyone was back to acting weird.

"You're welcome to use the classroom phone if you need to call home."

"I need *your* phone, actually." Alecia's eyes cut to her classmates.

Aaron shifted his weight to his other leg and gave them his best *I am willing to stand here for as long as it takes to get someone to raise their hand and answer* look. He had perfected this look— it was one of the reasons why he was able to get his classes to chat about history so much.

"Oh, just tell him," Morgan said.

Alecia looked at Morgan for a moment, then ducked her head and pulled a post-it note out of her binder. "We, um, made you a dating profile on the Single Professionals Match app."

She held the orange paper in his direction, but he didn't reach for it. "You... What?" He couldn't quite make sense of the words. "How did you even get my"— Then the previous class with these students came to mind. Four students were gone on the Young Ambassadors field trip and he didn't want them to get too far behind, so when the last half hour of the class turned to chatting, he'd let it turn into a bonding moment. "Now all the specific questions you were asking me on Friday make sense."

The kids were grinning. He couldn't ruin this for them just because he wasn't thrilled at all that they were trying to set him up too.

"You really got me to answer all the questions needed? How did you do it without a confirmation email coming to me?" He reached out and finally took the paper from Alecia.

"That was my genius idea," Cory said. "We just created a new email address for you."

"MrHallIsSingle at sentmail dot com," Kyle said.

Alecia pointed at the paper. "It's right there in your login information. The password to the email account is at the bottom."

"You might want to log in soon," Morgan said, sharing a grin with the rest of the class. "Your profile is pretty impressive. You've got quite a few interested people reaching out."

"Good-looking ones, too, Coach," Allen said.

"We've got your back," Alecia said. "We'll get you a wife by the end of the school year."

"That's our goal," Cory said.

Aaron rubbed his forehead with a thumb and two fingers, pretending like they were giving him a headache.

Which was completely and totally true, but he didn't want them to know that, so he made it obvious he was faking it. He didn't mind dating. He liked dating. Casual dating. It was the marriage part he wasn't okay with. He didn't need any more people trying to push him into it. "What am I going to do with you guys?"

"You could give us all A's for our troubles," Kyle said.

Like every kid in this class didn't already do everything necessary to earn A's.

"And bring us donuts on Thursday," Alecia said.

The last thing Aaron wanted was to be on a dating app. Their actions heaped frustration on top of frustration that seemed to come from every direction, but their hearts were in the right place. He might have to surprise them with donuts on Thursday just for being thoughtful.

Except that would probably only encourage them. He'd better not.

"Instead, how about I provide you with a feast of historical knowledge?" As he was writing *1450 to 1650: The Age of Discovery, Reconnaissance, Expansion* on the white board, the classroom on the other side of the wall erupted in cheers. "See? Even Mr. Klein's class agrees." The class gave half-hearted groans, but they dutifully pulled out their notebooks and held their pens or pencils at the ready, because if nothing else, this group of kids loved knowledge.

At the end of class, Aaron called out, "Morgan and Allen, I'll see you down at the pool in fifteen minutes for swim team practice. The rest of you, have a great Tuesday, and I'll see you in class on Thursday!"

As he stood at the door, giving each student a fist bump, hand shake, or high-five as they exited, Alecia said, "Mr. Hall, do you promise to install the app on your phone and see the people who are interested in you?"

Aaron took a deep breath. "I promise to think about it."

Alecia paused a moment like she was deciding if that was good enough, and then she nodded and left.

When the last student was gone, he walked over to his desk and stared down at the sticky note with the login information for his new email address and for Single Professionals Match. After a few moments, he opened his desk drawer, shoved the note in the back, shut the drawer, and walked out of his classroom.

————

By the time he left swim team practice, Aaron was mentally exhausted. Morgan and Allen had told the rest of his team — with great excitement — about setting their coach up on the dating app, and every single one of them was pressuring him to install it. He kept refocusing them on drills, and eventually on getting their form exactly right for the butterfly stroke, since that one wore them out the quickest, but they had been relentless in their coaxing.

He walked back to his classroom, put on his coat, got his bike out of his office, and wheeled it outside. He hadn't swum today, but he could still smell the chlorine on his slacks and button-down, which always happened simply by being in the same room as an indoor pool. The scent had been a near-constant companion since he'd first discovered swimming at age three, and for him, was tied to nearly every emotion a human could experience. It was a scent that made him feel more himself than anything else.

Normally, he would've gone for a swim after his team left to help wash away his frustration. But today's frustrations called for something different. He had never been one to drink— not after his first and only time a decade ago. He wasn't one to put less than wholesome things into his body for any reason, with one exception. And a day like today called for exactly that kind of self-medicating exception: ice cream. His students had told him about a great shop right in Nestled Hollow, so he figured he'd stop by before heading home to Mountain Springs.

As he rode his bike through the streets of the town, he tilted his face upward, letting the cold mountain scent wash over him as the wind got stronger the faster he pedaled. The wind rushing past him while biking always brought back the same sense of powerful speed that swimming brought him. That feeling of truly connecting all the senses in your body, your mind, and your muscles, with what was around you, and becoming all the more powerful because of it. It was intoxicating and exhilarating and made him feel invincible.

He slowed as he reached Main Street and turned on to the road. As he was heading to the other end of the street, a car pulled up next to him, matching his speed. He glanced over to see a student of his, Tim, and he waved.

Tim rolled down his window and said, "Hey, Mr. Hall. We've got a new hashtag trending. It's hashtag *NHH Finds a Wife For Mr Hall*. You should check it out!" Then the car pulled ahead and Tim rolled his window back up.

Aaron stopped pedaling and put his feet out as his bike stopped. Tim was one of his students, but he hadn't even had his class today. How had news spread so quickly? And how in the world was he going to stop something that had taken on a life of its own?

Needing the ice cream now even more than before, he spied With a Cherry on Top a couple of buildings down. He pedaled there, parked his bike in the rack out front, and went into the shop, the smell of sweet cream and sugary cones hitting him the second he walked in. If he was ever going to let himself have a vice, this would be it. Something about the smell of ice cream took him back to every good memory of his childhood. It didn't exactly make problems go away, but it helped.

"Do you already know what you'd like," a broad-shouldered man with a big voice said from behind the counter, "or can I interest you in a few sample spoons?"

Aaron leaned forward but realized that angle made his ankle injury from this morning hurt, so he shifted and looked at his choices. "Let's try *Maple, Please Bring Home the Bacon.*"

The man scooped out a bite on a little plastic spoon and handed it to Aaron. He put it in his mouth, and maple exploded across his tongue, the candied bacon and walnut adding the perfect amount of crunch. "Wow. Let's do a big scoop of that."

"You don't want to try any other flavors first?"

Aaron shook his head. "I don't care about anything else at the moment. This is all I'll be able to think of until I get a scoop. No wonder so many of my students recommended this place."

As the man scooped up his ice cream, Aaron's attention wandered around the shop. A dad and his two elementary school-aged kids sat at one table, and a woman holding a baby sat across from a woman with blonde curls that fell halfway down her back. The woman was chatting using her hands, a bunch of papers spread out in front of her, a cup of ice cream next to them. He turned back as the man handed him his ice cream, which had a cherry perched on top, just like on their logo. As he was paying, his eyes went back to the woman. There was something familiar about her.

"Enjoy," the man said.

Aaron turned to leave, but the woman caught his eye again.

Then an image of her awkwardly trying to brush the dirt off his coat hit him, and he smiled. They had met this morning. He walked over to her table. Just before he got there, a group of kids that all looked about ten years old, wearing matching basketball uniforms, walked in with their coach, and the woman with the baby stood up. As soon as she realized that Aaron was coming to her table, she said, "Oh, hi." Then she looked to the other woman, probably realizing that Aaron had come over because of her, and said, "Do you two know each other?"

The other woman's attention had been on her papers, spoon in hand. She looked at him like she was looking at a stranger, but only for a fraction of a second, then it turned to recognition and she nearly choked on her ice cream.

"Hi," he said. "Nice seeing you again. Especially under less painful circumstances." But as he was saying it, she had stood up so quickly that her chair fell over backward, hitting her in the shin, and she winced. So he added, "Or possibly equally painful circumstances."

"Oh hi. I, um, sorry about this morning. I'm so embarrassed. Lola isn't usually that crazy. Are you okay?

Did that, the wreck, do any damage? You know, to you or your bike?"

"We're both doing great, thank you for asking."

"I'm sorry. My brain is so deep in business planning I can't even think straight. But I am very sorry about this morning. Would you like to sit?"

He was about to open his mouth to say no, but between the number of tables and chairs in the shop and the number of kids on the basketball team, they'd probably all be taken, and riding a bike while holding an ice cream cone wasn't optimal. "Sure." He slung his coat over the back of the chair and sat down, then motioned to her ice cream cup. "What flavor did you go with?"

"My standby— *Is the Doctor Pepper In*? I see you went with *Maple, Please Bring Home the Bacon*. Quality choice, there."

"Well, I'm a quality guy, so it seemed appropriate."

She cocked her head to the side and narrowed her eyes as he took a bite. "What?" he asked around a mouthful.

"Just trying to figure this out."

He looked to the left and the right, suddenly self-conscious under her gaze.

"This isn't a celebratory ice cream for you."

"Nope." He took another bite.

"And you didn't just decide that ice cream was a viable choice for dinner tonight."

"Correct again."

She crossed her arms, studying him as he bit off another bite, this one giving him a brain freeze. "You're drowning your sorrows."

Aaron raised an eyebrow. "So, are you a professional Ice Cream Motivation Analyst?"

"Nah. The Professional Ice Cream Motivation Analyst Guild has exorbitant membership fees, so I decided to stay a hobbyist."

"Understandable. That's exactly the reason why I never joined the Professional Ice Cream *Eater's* Guild. So what about you? What's your ice cream reason today?"

She looked down at hers, picked up a spoonful, and put it in her mouth, a look of pure enjoyment on her face. "Celebration."

He held his ice cream cone out for a cheers, and she picked up her bowl and bumped it into his cone.

"So what are you celebrating?"

She sat up straighter in her chair and said, "I'm ignoring what everyone else wants me to do, and going six full months without dating."

Aaron thrust out his hand. "Hi, my name is Aaron Hall. Nice to meet you."

The woman laughed, then reached out and shook his hand. "Macie Zimmerman. I'm guessing we might have something in common."

MACIE

"So tell me," the man across from her said, as the chaos of kids on the basketball team all asked for sample spoons, "why are you choosing to go six months without dating?"

This was all still so new to her. She hadn't even thought about it much before she told Joselyn this morning, and now that she was telling this guy she just met, it felt like it was a commitment she was setting in stone. "Family is hugely important in my family. Well, it's hugely important to me, too. I would love to get married and have lots of kids, but I haven't found the right man to tie the knot with. And believe me, I've searched. Searching is exhausting mentally and emotionally, and I just need a break."

She lifted one shoulder in a shrug, and then

24

straightened the stack of papers in front of her. "There's a time for everything, and I feel like right now, it's time to focus on seeing if I can turn my business into something more. How about you?" She studied him, trying to read his body language and reading between the lines of what little he'd said. "I'm guessing you've got some reasons for not dating too."

He turned his cone around, studying his ice cream like it held all the answers. "My reasons have to do with where dating leads, and that is always to either a breakup or a marriage. And break ups get old after a while."

"And you don't see marriage in your future?"

"In *my* future? Not even a little bit."

"I'm sensing a story there, too."

He took a bite of his ice cream and chewed it slowly. "Trauma as a young adult, and a repeat as a slightly less-young adult. Not really an interesting story."

"And you're jaded. Don't forget that part."

He smiled, and his dimples were even visible through his scruff. They were cute. His brown scruff and matching short brown hair were cute, too. "You're a perceptive one, Macie Zimmerman."

"Only if you're eating ice cream. It kind of comes with the whole amateur Ice Cream Motivation Analyst gig." She ate a spoonful of hers. There was just nothing that paired better with ice cream than Dr. Pepper. First bite or the last, each one was exactly right. "So, do you have a 'no dating' pact too?"

"Before tonight I've pretty much had an 'always dating' pact, but after a day like I've had, going without sounds like an excellent idea. Why? Are you looking for an accountability partner? Is this going to be a hard commitment to keep if you don't have someone to report to?" He crunched into his cone.

She thought of everything not dating would entail, and suddenly she was worried it actually would be a hard commitment to keep. "I just wish I could get everyone off my back. Telling my parents isn't going to be fun. Not that they're controlling or anything, but they do know I want to get married and so they're going to think I'm making a terrible choice.

"And then there's the matter of my siblings and everyone in town always trying to set me up. Maybe I should have Whitney write an article in the Nestled Hollow Gazette with a big headline saying *Macie Zimmerman isn't dating for six months, so for the love of her sanity, don't set her up on any blind dates.* If I could get her to put it on the front page in big text, maybe people would listen."

Aaron laughed a big hearty laugh that made Macie chuckle. "Do you think she would add my name to that headline?"

"People in town are trying to set you up, too?"

He shook his head and licked the side of his cone. "I live in Mountain Springs. But I teach at Nestled Hollow High, and my students have made it their goal to get me married off by the end of the school year. And they're a pretty relentless bunch."

"No. They didn't." Macie laughed. She knew most of the high school students at NHH, and just imagining them being matchmakers to their teacher was the funniest thing she'd heard all day. She didn't mean to keep laughing, but she couldn't help it. "And I thought things were bad with my family and all the townspeople."

Aaron laughed, too. "You know, when one of my students said that hashtag *NHH Finds a Wife For Mr Hall* was trending, I didn't think it was so funny, but it really is."

Macie laughed even harder. The ten-year-olds were all getting their ice creams one by one and filling in the tables behind her. She pointed her spoon at the man. "See, what you need is a fake relationship. Get someone who will pretend to be your girlfriend, and then the students will feel like their job is done and back off."

Aaron froze, and then a grin spread across his face. "Not only are you the best amateur Ice Cream Motivation Analyst I've ever met, but you're also a brilliant genius. That would fix everything." He met her gaze, his eyes practically sparkling. "So are you up for the job?"

"Wait," Macie said. "Me? I wasn't meaning me." She

paused, blinking a few times. "You want me to be your fake girlfriend?"

"Sure! Why not? We're both in the same boat, so it's a win-win. I could get my students off my back and you could get your family and everyone else in town off your back. We could go on a couple of strategic fake dates, and then in a few months, we could break up. Our broken hearts would buy us at least three more months of people backing off. Then bam, you've got your six months, and I'll have made it to the end of the school year."

"Wow, I am kind of brilliant." She paused, searching his face. "But I don't know. That's just... I don't know."

"You want to get married and I never want to, so obviously the two of us would never work out as a couple. That's what makes this so perfect. No romantic feelings will get in the way— we'll just be two teammates working together for a common goal."

The more she thought about it, the more excited she became. This could be the answer she needed that she hadn't even known she was looking for. "Do you think it would work?"

The basketball team was all around the three other tables in the shop, all talking over one another and comparing ice cream flavors, raising the noise level and the excitement level in the room. The excitement started to bleed from them to her.

"Why not? How old are you?"

"Twenty-seven. You?"

"Twenty-nine. So pretty close. Plus we'd make an attractive couple."

Macie glanced at her sister and bit her lip. Could she keep a secret like this from her?

Aaron tipped his head in Joselyn's direction. "Who is that you're worried won't believe you?"

Macie chuckled that her face had been so easy to read. "My sister Joselyn. She knows we just met today."

"She's seen us having an engaging conversation. That usually precedes a date."

"True." Macie would have to keep it a secret from everyone else in her family, too. Could she do that? She was the one who obeyed the rules. She didn't lie. But the more she thought about it, the more sense it made. She could already feel the weight of the hope and disappointment that came along with dating lifting from her shoulders, and with that, she felt a smile lifting her face.

Macie pushed her ice cream off to the side, pulled the notebook from her stack of papers, opened it in front of her, and picked up her pen. "We need to figure out the details before we can enter into a contract."

"You aren't going to make me sign in blood, are you?"

"No, but we will need to head over to City Hall and have Gloria notarize it." She enjoyed the look of surprise on his face before she let him know she was kidding. But really, a part of her did want something more official than scribbles in her notepad.

"Okay, details," Aaron said. "We should probably each choose an event to show up together at that's going to give us the biggest bang for our buck. Oh! I've got it. Can I borrow your pen?"

Macie handed it to him, and he pulled a couple of napkins out of the holder that sat on their table and wrote something on it, hiding what he was writing. Then he folded it up in a fancy way that made it look like an envelope, completely surprising her that he knew how. He slid it across the table, a look of fabricated shyness on his face.

Macie picked it up, opened the "envelope," and read what he'd written out loud. "Will you go to Winter Formal with me? Ice cream if you'd say yes." The note took her right back to her high school days and she laughed. "Winter formal, huh?"

"I'm chaperoning. If we went together, all of my students would see. We'd be dressed fancy, which will make them go crazy for it. We could dance a few dances, and in their mind, the deal would be sealed. What do you think?"

When was the last time she had dressed up fancy? It might be fun to do it again. "When is Winter Formal?"

Aaron winced. "This Saturday. Is five days enough notice to get a dress?"

"Maybe." She took her pen back, pulled out her own napkin, wrote down her answer, folded it into a different envelope shape that she'd learned back in elementary school, and handed it to him.

After opening it, he read out loud, "'That sounds *sweet*. I won't leave you out in the *cold*— we were *mint* to go together.' Aww. My students would be so proud of this exchange here. I might have to tell the story in class. Okay, why would they not eat their cones?" he asked as he gestured with both hands toward the tables behind Macie. "The cone is practically the best part!" He took a big bite of his.

Macie turned to see what Aaron was looking at. All of the basketball kids had eaten the ice cream out of their cones and were putting them pointed side up on a tray, balancing more on top like a house of cards trying to be a castle. The noise level in the shop rose with each cone that they managed to put on top without falling.

Macie laughed at how much enjoyment the kids were getting from it, then turned and wrote *Aaron's strategic date: Winter Formal* on her paper, then tapped her pen on her lips, trying to decide what would be her best strategic date.

"My most strategic date would involve my family. How willing are you to go to a family thing with me? It might be the only way to convince them since if I really had a boyfriend, I'd bring him, no questions. My family has two parties— one on Christmas Eve that goes into Christmas Day, of course, but we also have a Christmas Kickoff get-together the weekend closest to when the twelve days of Christmas starts. It's the Saturday after the Winter Formal."

"That could be fun. Sure, why not?"

"I'm the youngest of seven kids."

Aaron's eyes grew wider.

"And they'll all be there."

She paused to let that sink in.

"And they're all married."

She waited, giving him a moment.

"And they all have kids."

It was comical how wide his eyes were getting. She ducked her head in apology. "Change your mind about this agreement? We haven't gone to Gloria to make it official, so it's not too late to back out."

Aaron swallowed hard and looked at his ice cream cone like it had betrayed him. Then he got up and threw it in the garbage can, then made his way back very slowly. She bit her lip, watching him, trying to guess exactly how awful that would be for him.

He sat back down, eyes on her, and said, "How many people are we talking?"

Macie looked up at the ceiling, doing the calculations in her head. "Thirty-three. Plus us."

"You've seriously got thirty-four people in your family,

just with you, your parents, and siblings on down? Without counting aunts or uncles or cousins?"

She nodded. "Why? How many do you have?"

"Four, including me. Unless you count the woman my dad married, then five." His eyes shifted to the chaos that the ten-year-olds were making as two of them were now trying to see who could smash their cones into bits the fastest. "So you're saying that a get-together at your house is kind of like that."

Macie winced.

"It's worse?"

"Well, that's like what? A dozen kids? We've got nineteen. Not that nineteen is much more than twelve, though," she added, hoping that it softened it a bit.

He sat up straighter in his chair. "Do you know what? I have one class with thirty-three students. I can do this. Write it down."

"Are you sure?"

"I'm asking you to get a dress on extremely short notice. It's the least I can do."

She wrote down *Macie's strategic date: Family Christmas Kickoff party*. "We might need a couple more dates just to make sure it's believable. Should we just say that we'll keep the number even between yours and mine?"

Aaron nodded.

"Sorry to interrupt."

Macie jumped at her sister's comment. She hadn't noticed her coming.

"The night crew just got here," Joselyn said, "so we thought we'd head over to Snowdrift Springs Park and see if they need any help with decorating the city tree before the lighting. Do you want to join us?" Her eyes cut to Aaron. "You could bring your friend."

Macie's and Aaron's eyes met, and he raised an eyebrow, asking if she wanted to go. "It might make Saturday go more smoothly if we've already been somewhere together."

"True," Macie said, even though it would make the fake relationship thing go from theoretically a good plan to real-life scary and committed, even though she hadn't had nearly enough time to consider all the angles enough to commit yet. She didn't take leaps like this. But, she told herself, this wasn't a leap. This was taking the safe way around to *avoid* leaps. She studied him for a moment and then turned to her sister. "Emily is closing up Paws and Relax and taking care of the animals, so I'm good there, but I'll still need to stop by after to get Lola and Reese. But we'd love to."

"What's Saturday?" Joselyn asked.

This was the moment. She'd have to commit to it fully if she was going to convince Joselyn. "We," Macie said, smiling at Aaron, "have a date."

AARON

Aaron had been teaching at Nestled Hollow High for more than three months, but he realized that all of his time spent in Nestled Hollow had been at the high school, or, on the very rare occasion, grabbing a quick bite to eat. He'd quickly fallen in love with the students there and he had the time, so he'd volunteered for nearly every after-school assignment the school offered.

But all of that— every swim meet, school dance, football game, band competition, drama production, tennis match, and soccer game— had been on campus. He'd spent almost no time at all in the town itself.

Come to think of it, he hadn't spent much time at town functions in Mountain Springs either. Or in Colorado Springs before that. So the tree decorating caught him a little off guard.

The lighting itself wasn't until six, and that's when everyone showed up, but there were still at least three dozen people there, helping to decorate the giant tree smack dab in the middle of the park. It stood several feet taller than all the others and looked like it had probably been there since before Nestled Hollow was even a town.

Macie seemed excited by the event, and she was trying to get him excited, too. True, he spent most of his time with high school students and adults, but families came to NHH sporting events, so it wasn't like he wasn't used to crowds like this. Maybe it was just because as a kid, his life had revolved around swimming, school, and his sister's dance competitions. Going to town events just wasn't in his family's DNA.

"We should help them decorate," Macie said.

Several high ladders were evenly spaced around the tree, and the city had one of their cranes with a basket at the end to hold a person that was extended to the top of the tree. There were several people on each ladder, standing at different heights, and people were passing ornaments up, assembly-line style.

"I'm not sure we're supposed to," Aaron said. "Besides, it looks like they've got it under control."

She gave him a smile that clearly said she thought that was a flimsy excuse, and pulled him toward the totes of ornaments along with Joselyn, Joselyn's husband, and their baby. The people in charge must have been okay with everyone helping because nobody stopped them. And it was actually a lot of fun— he was glad that Macie had made him participate.

The darker it got, the more families arrived. Not too many teens had been at the decorating part, but more and more of them were coming in anticipation of the lighting. At 5:45, they took down the ladders and set up a microphone and a small platform. People started finding spots in front of the tree.

"It's getting pretty cold. I think I'll go grab my bike from in front of the ice cream shop and head home."

"You can't leave," Macie said. "They haven't lit the tree yet."

He glanced up at it. "This isn't my thing. I've seen a couple of students already, and the rumor mill will probably take it from here."

"Have you never seen a big tree lighting before?" When he shook his head, Macie said, "It's incredible. It's nothing like a tree in your living room. It took Sam three full days to get this many lights wound onto the tree. Stay. It'll change your life."

He raised an eyebrow in challenge.

"Think I'm wrong? The only way to prove it is to stay."

"Perceptive *and* persistent." He took a deep breath, looked up at the tree, and then glanced at the crowds pulling up in the parking lot or walking toward the park, all bundled up in their winter clothes. Some of them were certainly his students. And after helping to decorate the tree, he found himself wanting to see how it would look lit up. "Okay, I'll stay."

She led him to an area in front of the tree near the microphone, on the side that people coming from the parking lot would reach first, and they both rubbed their hands together to keep warm. Not two minutes passed, and he could already see a handful of more students. Morgan and LeeAnn headed straight for them.

Macie slipped her hand into his. He turned to her and smiled. "Nice touch." She grinned back at him.

"Hi, Coach Hall! Hi, Macie!" Morgan said as the two girls from his AP class neared. He caught the moment that both girls' eyes flicked to their hands and then back up to their faces.

Aaron looked from Morgan to Macie. "You two know each other?"

"Well, duh," Morgan said. "We do live in the same town. And she gives me puppy therapy. I swear I wouldn't have made it through finals at the end of last year if it wasn't for her."

LeeAnn nodded her agreement. "And without her, I never would've been able to handle breaking up with Peter."

"If it weren't for Macie opening Paws and Relax, we'd both be blubbering piles of Morgan and LeeAnn-colored goo on the ground."

"It's true," LeeAnn said. "She, like, literally saves lives."

"Wow. A life-saver and an all-but-pro Ice Cream Motivation Analyst. You are one talented woman." How had they decided to commit to a fake relationship, and he hadn't once even thought to ask what she did for a living? That was the kind of thing a boyfriend would know. He needed a crash course in Macie Zimmerman.

"Don't forget perceptive and persistent," Macie said.

He smiled. "I'm pretty sure I couldn't forget that if I tried."

"So you two are dating?" Morgan asked. "When did this happen?"

Well," Aaron said, "we first met this morning, actually. It was a pretty explosive meeting, like a bolt came out of nowhere and knocked me right off my feet. With such a memorable meeting, I couldn't stop thinking about her all day long. One thing led to another, so we met at With a Cherry on Top"—

"Where he knocked me off my feet just as quickly"—

"And we had an amazing conversation and just really hit it off."

Macie looked up at him and smiled. "By the time we finished an *Is the Doctor Pepper In?* and a *Maple, Please Bring Home the Bacon*, we had decided that life would be perfect if we started dating."

LeeAnn put both of her hands over her heart. "Oh my goodness, that is the sweetest story I've heard in my life!"

Macie reached out and placed her fingers on his biceps. "It doesn't stop there, girls. He even asked me to Winter Formal."

Both girls squealed in delight.

Morgan glanced at the choir. "Oh! We've got to get up there quickly." She grabbed LeeAnn's wrist, and started backing toward the choir while calling out, "But we want to hear all about this in class on Thursday!"

This was working even more perfectly than he could have possibly hoped. Macie was pulling it off beautifully. As the chatting from the crowd grew, he leaned in and whispered in her ear, "You are amazing, teammate. That went beyond what I had hoped for. And pulling it off in front of those two was especially perfect."

Macie turned and put her lips right next to his ear and said, "And I'm pretty sure that you leaning in to whisper in my ear like that just set the rest of the town abuzz. Nice work, teammate."

He stole a glance behind them and sure enough, everyone was watching them, even Macie's sister and her family. Smiling, he turned back as Macie pressed her side into his, blocking the fist she raised from everyone's view behind them. He bumped his fist into hers as they grinned at each other. "We've got this."

A man stepped up to the microphone, and the crowd quieted. Macie leaned closer and said, "That's Mayor Stone."

"Welcome to the one hundred fifty-fourth annual lighting of the town Christmas tree! I think a lot of you remember when this beauty was a little shorter and a little easier to decorate," he said, putting his hand on one of the lower branches of the tree and looking up at its height. "She's all grown up now, so we decided she needed a few more lights than she had before. This year, it's an unprecedented thirteen thousand seven hundred lights!"

Everyone around cheered, so Aaron joined them and clapped.

"Now the Nestled Hollow High choir's here," the mayor said, "and they've got a special number for us. When they're finished, we'll flip the switch and watch the magic happen!"

"I'm ready for my life to be changed," Aaron said as the choir started singing. "I hope you weren't just using hyperbole on me."

"I stand by my hyperbole. It comes with a Macie Money Back Guarantee."

As the choir sang *Do You Hear What I Hear*, Aaron found himself swaying back and forth slightly, along with the rest of the town. Like they were all Whos down in Whoville. He immediately stopped swaying.

The choir did sound pretty amazing, though. It was great to see so many of his students singing—he was used to only seeing them at school events.

They all sang louder as they neared the end. "He will

bring us goodness and light." They held out the last word so long that he was so proud of the lung capacity of all of his swim team members in the group. As the conductor motioned to cut off the song and the last sounds of the word "light" faded into the mountains, the lights of the Christmas tree lit up the entire park. Aaron had to admit that it was one of the most beautiful displays of light he had ever seen.

And with a loud bang from somewhere across town, everything went dark.

Amidst the surprised murmurs and exclamations from the crowd, someone called out, "Looks like you made it a little *too* unprecedentedly awesome!"

"Well," someone else said, "we now know what our maximum awesome is. I guess we need to dial it back."

"Nonsense," the mayor said. "We've never dialed it back before, and we're not about to on my watch. Folks, it looks like we managed to flip the breaker, of sorts. I know this is a huge disappointment for everyone, and that you all had hoped to be reveling in the beauty of the tree, but don't you worry. As you can see, Sam has already taken off running to go see if he can find and fix the problem. Now help yourself to some refreshments over here, and we'll hurry to get some lamps set up so you can see what you're eating."

Joselyn neared with her husband and baby and Macie asked them, "Are you guys staying for refreshments?"

The husband— Aaron was going to have to find out his name soon— answered, "Of course! Power's out to our houses, anyway, so no sense going home. What about you two?"

Aaron looked at Macie. "I've got a twelve-mile bike ride ahead of me. I think I better grab my bike and head home."

Macie shivered in the cold, probably thinking about how much colder the wind made a bike ride when the temperatures were low like this. "It's so dark! Do you want a ride home? I've got a brother with a truck. He's probably here somewhere with his family. We could put your bike in the back and I could drive you."

He smiled. "Nah. I do this kind of thing all the time, so I'm prepared. I've got a great headlight, warm clothes, and a path I could follow with my eyes closed."

"I'm going to head over with him," Macie said. "I'll grab Reese and Lola from the shop while I'm there— I'll see you all back at home."

As they walked back to the far end of Main Street where he'd left his bike outside of With a Cherry on Top, Aaron and Macie chatted about how it went and about the dance. The news that the students were going to band together to find him a wife had spread so quickly, he was interested to see how fast the rumors that he was dating Macie would spread. He could barely wait for school tomorrow to find out.

As they passed Paws and Relax, the dog that had caused his bike wreck this morning and the other big dog that Macie had with her raced to the front windows, their barking muffled behind the glass. Macie waved at them and gave them some kind of hand signal. He remembered from what LeeAnn and Morgan had said that this was her business, so he at least knew that about her.

"Oh! Phone numbers!" Macie said as she pulled out her phone and unlocked the screen. She opened her contacts and handed him her phone.

He did the same and handed his to her. She took a picture of herself first and then started entering her information. Aaron thought of following suit, but the truth was, he hadn't perfected the art of taking selfies, so he just put in his name and phone number.

He switched phones back and looked down at the information Macie had put in his contacts for her. The picture drew his eyes first. With all the power out in the town, she was lit only by the silver moonlight, and it made the picture look like it was in black and white. Instead of looking at the camera, she was looking off into the distance, looking for something or someone in the dark.

Then he noticed her contact information. "Macie 'My Mysterious Goddess' Zimmerman?"

She smiled and lifted one shoulder in a shrug. "In case I call or text and one of your students sees it." She glanced down at her phone. "Aaron 'Dashing Man' Hall."

Aaron burst out laughing, and Macie quickly joined him. The truth was, he'd never entered his contact information like that into a woman's phone before. But it had somehow felt right in this fake relationship of his.

"Text me the details about the dance," Macie said as Aaron grabbed his helmet off his handlebars and fastened it on his head.

"Will do." He swung a leg onto his bike and flipped on the headlight. "And I'll start preparing myself for the onslaught of your family a week from Saturday."

"Throwing yourself into the chimpanzee enclosure at the zoo might help with that."

Aaron chuckled nervously. "Good to know."

MACIE

M acie practically skipped from task to task as she took care of the animals at Paws and Relax the next morning. Last night had been fun. This fake relationship thing was one of the better ideas she'd ever had. When Joselyn got back home, she found out that four of her siblings had been at the tree lighting, and they had seen her and Aaron together. They had pulled everything off so well that they all thought she was dating someone new.

She'd been worried about whether or not she'd be able to convince her sister. But Joselyn knew that when Macie first started dating someone, before she figured out for herself what she thought of him, she didn't like talking about it. Macie always needed to get things figured out in her own mind first. Chatting as both sisters and best friends with Joselyn, getting excited about all the little things the guy she was interested in did— that came later. The precedent she had set worked in her favor this time because she hadn't had a lot of practice in fooling people.

Emily, her one and only employee, didn't have any college classes today and was more than happy for the extra hours (and the extra time with the animals) that Macie offered her by coming in today. Once all the animals were fed and petted and played with and cared for, Emily walked in. Macie filled her in on the schedule for today— a Parent, Preschooler, and a Puppy weekly event in an hour, the open Pet a Pet hour during lunch, where anyone could drop in to get a boost and a bit of relaxation, and the daily Chill After School session. Then she headed into her office, closed her door, and spread her business plans across her desk.

And then she remembered about the dance. She pulled out her phone and texted Brooke, the woman who owned Best Dressed, a shop on Main Street that sold fancy dresses. She took a deep breath, and then decided it was time to start planting more seeds about her's and Aaron's budding "relationship."

> Macie: Hi, Brooke! I started dating a man who asked me to accompany him as he chaperones Winter Formal at the high school on Saturday. I know it's short notice, but any chance you still have a dress available?

Brooke's response came quickly.

Brooke: Yes! I have the perfect one for you. And you're in luck because I just stepped off a plane three days earlier than I had planned. Can you come to the shop at 4?

Macie: You are a godsend. See you at 4!

She pressed *send* and then got to work on her plans.

It felt good to pour all her focus into her business. Everything went so well when she was with the animals. This— her business and the pets— was all she needed in her life.

She spent the day brainstorming ways to let more people experience the joy of these animals, especially the dogs. After several hours, she had what she thought was a great list of ideas.

She had a one-page listing of birthday party packages, where she'd team up with her sister's and brother-in-law's shop for ice cream at the end. She'd come up with different packages, along with their prices and what they offered, and she'd even come up with a list of games that would involve the dogs, a treasure-hunting game to find the lost cat toys (since they were always lost within moments of finding them anyway), and time to play with and hold the animals. She had a party package where she would take the dogs to the birthday boy's or girl's house or a park, with her or Emily running the party.

She had a field trip plan for the local elementary and middle school science classes, with information about each type of animal, and what instantly became her favorite: a program where people could rent-a-pet for an hour or an afternoon or evening, so they could enjoy a pet in their own home. She hoped people would see how much they enjoyed it, and think about adopting their own rescue pet.

Each item would take a lot of time and effort to get graphic images, signage for her shop, her website updated, and advertising. She had her work cut out for her. But the dogs were good dogs who loved being around people. It made her happy thinking of how much they'd enjoy more time to play and be loved and take a nap in someone's lap.

If all these plans went well, though, she might be able to make enough each month to justify putting an offer on the building. Except that was such a huge commitment that part of her worried she'd never be able to make the choice in the amount of time she had.

Her stomach grumbled, and she lit up her phone to see the time. No wonder she was so hungry! She had worked through lunch, and it was almost time to meet Brooke to look at dresses. After organizing all her new plans into a nice stack, she hurried out of her office. A half-dozen elementary school-aged kids, including one of her nephews, were playing with the dogs, cat, and hamsters, a couple of high school students were brushing Reese's fur, and one had a cat asleep in her lap.

"Everything going well?" Macie asked Emily.

"Sam went into her crazy cat ninja mode for a bit and alarmed Cookie and a couple of kids, but that only lasted about twenty seconds before she plopped down in front of Brandon here, looking to be petted. Other than that, we've been doing great!"

"Are you okay to run things until I get back? And then I'll stay until time to close things up."

"No problem. Oh, hey— I heard you were dating someone! Why didn't you tell me last night?"

This wasn't normal dating, so it was time Macie stopped doing her normal "don't say anything until you decide how much you like him" responses. She agreed to this fake relationship so that people would stop setting her up on dates or saying who she'd be perfect for, so she might as well take full advantage of the plan.

She smiled big. "His name is Aaron, and he teaches history at the high school, and he's pretty amazing, actually, and that's all I'm going to say about that." Then she ducked her head, which she hoped came across like she was a little shy talking about it, instead of the truth, which was that she wasn't sure how well she pulled off the lie, and she just realized that the high school students were listening in.

Emily squealed, and out of the corner of her eye, she could see that the high school students were silently squealing as if she couldn't tell that they were eavesdropping. "I've got to run. Have fun!" she called out to the room, and then raced out the door.

This would get easier, right? The more people she told, the more comfortably it would come. She just needed to think thoughts of her ideal man before talking and pretend that she'd finally found him. She crossed over the creek that ran down the middle of Main Street at the Center Street bridge and went into Best Dressed near the middle of the block.

A bell rang on the door when she walked in. Even with the dance just three days away, there were still a few dresses and tuxes in the shop. As she waited for someone to come up to the front, Macie wandered toward the dress side and looked at a few of them. They all had the *By the Brooke* tag on the inside of the neck with Brooke's company logo and were all beautiful. She glanced at one of the price tags. She was a good saver, but with the uncertainty about her business, she was nervous about spending so much.

"Macie!" Brooke said as she came from somewhere in the back to the store at the front. "I swear it feels like I've been gone for a month. It's good to see you! Come on back."

"Oh, we're not looking at"— Macie motioned to the

dresses in the store as Brooke grabbed her hand and led her toward the back rooms.

"No, those aren't for you. So I've only been back in town for like two seconds, but long enough to hear that you and your new man are 'so cute' together."

"It's true," Macie said. "We're a 'downright delightful' couple."

Brooke laughed. "This town really does get excited about things like this, don't we? That's why I only go on dates with people in other states."

Macie had never been in the back rooms of Best Dressed. It was easily four times the size of the front, and Brooke's two employees stood around a big design table, discussing a pattern in front of them. She was pretty sure that one of the women lived in Denver and commuted here. The other woman moved to Nestled Hollow not long ago, but Macie didn't know her. Bolts of fabric hung on the walls, and 3 sewing machines sat at big tables. It looked like there were a few offices in the back. She waved at the other two women, and they smiled back.

Brooke turned and studied Macie. "Really, though, you look happy. Are you happy?"

Macie smiled thinking about it. She was happy about how everything was working out. She channeled that in her answer. "I am. It's new and fun and I'm enjoying it."

"Good to hear. Now, are you looking to keep or return?"

At first, Macie thought Brooke was talking about Aaron, and a pang of worry hit her that Brooke had seen beyond their facade. Then, probably at Macie's confused face, she reworded it. "Do you want to borrow or buy?"

"Oh! You loan dresses?"

"Not usually. Only to you, actually. You only need it for a few hours on Saturday, right? I know you're looking into possibly buying your building, and I'm guessing you'd rather not have an unexpected expense right now. Yes?"

Macie let out a huge breath. "Brooke, when I said you were a godsend, I clearly was minimizing your amazingness."

"Well, you, my fellow single businesswoman," Brooke said, holding a swatch of fabric up by her face, "are freaking adorable and I've always wanted to dress you in one of my gowns."

Macie drew back in surprise. "For real? Why?"

Brooke smiled. "And that's just one of the ways in which you're adorable."

Macie didn't have long to be confused before more questions came her way. "Do you have a color preference? Style preference?"

"Honestly, I haven't dressed up fancy or even thought about dressing up fancy for so long, I don't even know what my preferences are."

"Can I choose then? I have one I designed with you in mind."

"*Me* in mind? I don't understand."

Brooke walked to a door at the back half of the building as she talked, and Macie followed her. "With every dress I design, I have a certain person in mind. I figure that person represents a slice of the population. If I am designing with that specific person and their personality in mind, it should resonate with the slice of the world that person represents."

Macie's phone dinged, and she pulled it out as Brooke went through her racks of dresses. It was a text from Aaron.

> Aaron: Hello, my mysterious goddess. The dance starts at 8:30, and they need chaperones there at 8.

Macie smiled and typed in her response.

> Macie: Sounds great, my dashing man. I will meet you at the high school at 8:00 then.

"Mysterious goddess, huh?" Brooke said and Macie jumped. She hadn't even noticed that Brooke had come back out of the room.

Macie blushed, and then looked back down when her phone dinged. She almost slipped it into her pocket without replying, but then Brooke said, "No— reply. Don't keep Dashing Man waiting." So Macie opened Aaron's text, read it, and replied.

> Aaron: Do you know what color your dress is yet? I just want to make sure we look incredible together.

> Macie: I'm finding out right now.

> Macie: P.S. We'll look incredible together even if our outfits go together about as well as eating peanuts and chewing gum.

> Aaron: True. Okay then, I'll wear bright bold stripes; you wear lumberjack plaid.

> Macie: Deal.

"Are you ready to see it?" Brooke asked, a zipped garment bag lying over her arm.

Macie had *thought* she was ready. But it hit her that Brooke wasn't letting Macie choose— she was giving her exactly one dress to try on. What if she hated it? She didn't want to hurt Brooke's feelings, especially since she was so willing to help her out with such short notice.

But she also didn't want a repeat of her own disastrous Winter Formal, where she wore a dress handed down through both of her sisters and had a seam in an essential place that she didn't know was one fast song away from bursting open. She put a smile on her face and said, "Yep!"

Brooke hung it on a nearby rack, then unzipped the white bag and pulled out a royal blue gown that was the most stunning thing Macie had ever laid her eyes on. The satin straps lay just off the shoulders, and fell to a V at the neck, just above exquisite beading through the bodice. The skirt was full, but not gathered as much in the front, giving it a more sleek look while still being worthy of a ball.

"Brooke," Macie breathed. "How...how did you know?" She hadn't even known what her perfect formal dress would look like before this moment.

A smile spread across Brooke's face as she ushered her into the room with the racks of clothes. "I told you I'm good at reading people. Now go try it on. I'll help you zip it up."

As soon as Brooke closed the door, Macie slipped off her jeans and sweater and stepped into the dress. The fabric Brooke had used on the lining made the dress feel more incredible against her skin than anything she had ever worn. She opened the door and moved her hair to one side so Brooke could zip it up.

Brooke pulled at several spots along the bodice, testing to see if it needed any adjustments, but it seemed perfect in every way already. "Come see," Brooke said and led

Macie to a full-length mirror that was easily four times as wide as her mirror at home.

Macie ran her hands down the front of the dress. There was nothing about it that wasn't exactly right in every way. Dreaming up a dress this incredible wasn't even something her brain was capable of. "Brooke, I always thought you were a pretty cool person. But I had no idea that you were a mind-reading savant. A couture genius. Amazing beyond words."

"Stop it," Brooke said. "It's all you. I could design a dress out of a tarp and sew it with my eyes closed and you'd still look good in it."

Macie rolled her eyes.

"Don't let her downplay herself," Brooke's employee said. "There's a reason I'm willing to drive this far every day to come work with her. She's brilliant."

Brooke blushed and waved away the comment. "So, do you think it'll work? A lot of the girls buy their dresses here, so knowing what they bought, I think it will fit in with the others at the Winter Formal, but it won't make you look like a student."

"I know that every high school student wants to look like a princess at Winter Formal. This dress, though," Macie turned to each side, and then turned to see it from the back, "it makes me feel like a queen." She found herself standing taller and with more presence just wearing it.

Her phone's text alert started going off, text after text in quick succession. She had her phone on silent, and she only had two people on emergency bypass—Joselyn and Emily. She gathered up her skirt and raced back to the room where she'd changed, and pulled her phone out of the pocket of her jeans. The texts were from Emily.

> Emily: Chaos Here

The next text was a picture of the front area of Paws and Relax with kids and pets running all around, some kind of white substance scattered everywhere. Was that stuffing from one of the sitting pillows? She zoomed in. No, it was toilet paper. It had to be several rolls' worth, strung everywhere and torn to pieces.

> Emily: Come help?

Macie sent a quick *On my way* text.

"Let me help unzip you," Brooke said as she stepped up behind her. "It looks like they need you quickly—I can have the dress packaged and ready for you to pick up after work."

"Thank you. For all of this."

"You just make sure you have fun Saturday. Hopefully, your date will go more smoothly than that," Brooke said as she nodded at Macie's phone and winked.

six

AARON

Aaron worried it might be hard to convince his class that he and Macie were dating, but he'd barely had to even tell them. By Wednesday morning, the rumors were in full swing, especially since they all seemed to know Macie. Since he didn't live in Nestled Hollow, he hadn't even thought to consider the small-town everyone-knows-everyone thing. This fake relationship thing was going to be a cake walk.

As the week went on and the buzz of excitement from the students about Winter Formal grew, he found himself getting excited, too. He had already chaperoned the Homecoming and Sadie Hawkins dances, so he knew he'd enjoy himself, but he had to admit that he was more excited knowing that he was taking Macie this time. She seemed fun. And he was quite enjoying being on the same team as her in this game they were playing.

For a small moment earlier in the week, he'd contemplated calling around to some costume shops in Denver to see if they had any suits for rent that had bright bold stripes, if for no other reason than he thought Macie would get a kick out of it. But when she texted saying that her dress was blue, he changed his mind. Instead, he put on a crisp white shirt, a tie with a royal and navy blue pattern, and his favorite black dress suit.

Which just happened to have royal blue pinstripes.

Thanks to his quick thinking to get a haircut on Wednesday so it had a few days to get to that just right length, and a fresh trim of his scruff, he had to admit he looked pretty good in his formalwear.

He looked down at his watch. He'd made sure he was ready to go in the mirror of the faculty restroom, and it was now two minutes to eight, so Macie should be arriving any moment. He should get down to the gym to check-in.

He had been joking around with the Polanskis, a married couple who both worked at the high school— him as a counselor and her as the Spanish teacher— who were the other chaperones for the night, when he caught movement from the corner of his eye. He turned just as Macie walked into view and he lost the ability to talk. She was all smiles as they walked toward each other and he was all— he wasn't sure. Gaping-mouthed, probably. As they met in the middle, the "you look lovely" he had planned to say never made it to his lips as he took in how amazing she looked.

No, amazing didn't begin to cover it. Words that were never part of his spoken vocabulary filled his mind. Words like *splendor* and *grace* and *brilliance*. All those words translated into a choked, "That is very much not lumberjack plaid."

Macie laughed. "And those stripes are far from bright and bold."

"I guess everyone's just going to have to deal with us being the best-looking couple here." Aaron winked and Macie laughed like she thought he was joking. But even if he was the least attractive person in the room, with the two of them averaged together, they'd still win. "Come here— I've got something for you."

He led her to the refreshments table next to the Polanskis and opened the box he had sitting there. Macie's face lit up. "You even got me a corsage?"

"What kind of high school dance date would I be if I didn't?" He grinned as he slipped it on her wrist.

The lights dimmed, music started playing, and someone flipped on the hundreds and hundreds of clear Christmas lights that were placed in the fake snow that decorated the edges of the gym, wound around the archway where the photographer set up to take couples and group pictures, and hung from the refreshment tables. Another switch was flipped, and projected images of snowflakes filled the ceiling. A few at a time, students started trickling into the room.

"I haven't even thought of school dances in so long!" Macie said. "I forgot how magical dim lights, music, and cheesy decorations can make the gym."

Back when he'd chaperoned his first dance at Bunnell High in Colorado Springs, he learned pretty quickly that kids didn't go out for a smoke or try to spike the punch or sneak off to make out in a dark hallway if he interacted with them. So he and Macie went from group to group around the room, chatting with kids. They held hands the whole time, and that little detail didn't go unnoticed by the students. Macie was great with them, too. She had a way of making them feel important.

"There's a group of girls over there who came stag," Macie said as they walked along the outside of the dance floor. "They look like they want to dance."

"And there's a group of boys over there who look afraid to dance. Shall we give them both a nudge?"

"Three, two, one, and break," Macie said as she released his hand and headed toward the girls. He went the other direction and met up with the boys.

He chatted with the boys, asking them easy questions until they started giving him more than one-word answers.

Then he asked them if they came there to dance. Every single one of them found a random object nearby suddenly very fascinating to look at.

"Come on, guys. I know you don't want to go home having not taken the chance to dance with someone. See that group of girls over there?" He turned to point out the girls. Macie already had them out on the dance floor, all of them dancing to the fast beat. She gave him an encouraging thumbs up. "They'd love to dance and are just waiting for you to ask. So go ask one of them. If you get turned down, at least you won't go home feeling bad about not trying. And who knows? You might have a great time."

A few of the boys started walking toward them, then halted when they sensed that their friends weren't all coming, and turned back around. "Shoulders back, deep breath," he said to the few stragglers. "Now go be brave."

He smiled as all seven of the boys headed toward the group of girls. As he and Macie met in the middle, all the boys were dancing in the same group as the girls. Some got into it a little more than others, who just kind of bounced in place.

"Nice work," she said.

"You too." As the fast beat came to an end, a slow song began to play, and the now bigger group of stag students started asking each other to dance. "What do you think? Should we join them?"

She held out her hand. He took it in his and wrapped

his other arm around her waist as she wrapped hers around his shoulder and they began to move. Aaron had dated a fair amount in his life, but he didn't go dancing often. The last time he asked a date to join him as a chaperone, things had gone horribly wrong. "Now, admittedly, I haven't gone dancing with a ton of people since high school, so the pool of competition isn't huge, but you're possibly the most graceful person I've danced with."

Macie gave a little curtsey as they danced. "You aren't half bad yourself."

"You can thank my parents for that— it's not a choice that I would've initially made myself. I grew up swimming competitively, and my parents read somewhere that if your child is in a sport where a lot of precision is required, they'll do better if they also train in ballroom dance. So I joined my high school team."

"And did it help?"

Aaron shrugged a shoulder. "Probably. Hard to say."

"I joined ballroom for an entirely different reason."

Aaron's eyebrow lifted in surprise. "So your parents didn't tell you that your cell phone privileges would be revoked if you didn't join?"

Macie laughed. "Nope. They couldn't have. I didn't get my first cell phone until after graduation. I had been taking dance since I was two, though, so I figured moving from dancing solo or in a group to dancing with a partner wouldn't be too much of a stretch. Not that I was interested in ballroom per se—but I was interested in Ezra Knight. Based on our heights, I knew we'd get paired together, and I figured it would be the perfect way to get him to notice me."

"Did it work?"

She nodded. "It did. Kind of hard not to notice a person when you've got your arms around them or are lifting them in the air."

Aaron managed to choke on his saliva and coughed a few times in his attempt to recover. "Yeah, you could say that." He was acutely aware of exactly how Macie's waist felt under his hand and trying not to let it affect his ability to think. Or to swallow without choking. "But no happily ever after to the story, huh?"

Macie shook her head. "I mean, there was for a while. Then I had work after practice one day, so I got changed quickly and walked into the gym where the boys were hanging out together, long before they were expecting any of us. And Ezra Knight was leading a discussion where they were all ranking various body parts of all the girls."

"Ouch."

"Yeah, it was a bit of a crush squasher, so I only stayed on the team for a year. But I got some valuable ballroom dance practice out of the deal. I can now do a pretty mean cha-cha. Or at least I could back in tenth grade."

The song ended then, and Aaron released Macie. The

next song had a much faster beat. After a few seconds of listening, he said, "How about the fox trot? Think we could do it to this song?"

Macie took another step back, finger tapping her lip, looking at him but studying the music, her head bopping to the beat. The more she listened, the bigger a smile spread across her face. She lifted her skirt a bit a few times like she was testing how much movement she would have before she finally nodded. She put her arms up in the air and moved her hips to the beat, then did a few twirls around him as he stood still. Excitement bubbled up in Aaron, and a smile spread across his face.

She reached her arms out straight and put both hands on one shoulder, then one in the air. Aaron twirled around once, and then they both started into the footwork. Slow, slow, quick, quick. Slow, slow, quick, quick. He was rusty, but it was coming back to him faster than he thought it would.

He reached out for Macie's hand and she twirled into him, and then they twirled around together. Then Macie stepped out, arms outstretched as he did, and they switched spots, circling each other, stretching their arms out like it was a dance they'd rehearsed dozens of times. She put her hand on his neck and he put his hand on her back, and they swung around, other arm outstretched.

They moved across the floor, using the footwork he'd

learned so long ago, one hand on each other's shoulder, elbows high, other hands clasped outstretched. When they reached the other side, Macie kicked her leg up as he leaned her back. They added so many flourishes to the dance as they went, matching each other so well, he wasn't sure who was leading whom anymore. They just moved to the music and the movement of each other. They moved from side to side, touching, releasing, touching, releasing.

As the song neared the end, he held her close and spun them both together, Macie's leg rose behind her. At the last note of the song, she leaned back on his arm, and he lowered her into an impressive dip and she held it, arm outstretched.

He pulled her back to standing, and they stood chest to chest, breathing heavy, laughing breaths. Macie was practically glowing, and he suspected he was looking pretty happy himself. He wasn't sure he had ever enjoyed himself that much on a date before. "If high school ballroom had been anything like this, my parents wouldn't have had to force me to go."

"If I'd have had a partner like you, I'd have stayed on the team as a junior and senior, too. I haven't had this much fun dancing in years!"

The cheering around them finally caught Aaron's attention, and he noticed for the first time exactly how many people had cleared the dance floor, making a circle of spectators around them. He spun Macie out, and with their hands still clasped and their breathing still ragged, they lifted their arms in the air, and then took a deep bow.

The next song was another fast-paced song, and the students surrounding them looked ready to dance, so he called out, "And that was our portion of the dance-off. Now show us what you've got!" Then he led Macie to the refreshments table and grabbed them both a cup of punch.

"That was incredible," he said after taking a swallow. "*You* are incredible."

Macie gulped down her punch then said, "You were pretty incredible yourself."

Looking at Macie now, he realized he was admiring much more than the way she looked in that dress. There was something about this girl that was unlike anyone he'd ever dated—fake or real—before. She was fun and talented and beautiful and amazing with the students and made him feel alive. And having his hand on her waist, in her hand, and dropping her into a dip was electrifying. Not to mention the way it felt to have her hand on his neck or her arm on his shoulder.

But then he reminded himself that what they both wanted out of life was at complete odds with one another. She wanted the spouse and children. He didn't. The kids all around them in this room—they were his kids. He cleared his throat and motioned at the students. "And look what we started."

Macie turned to watch as all the students were on the dance floor, dancing and cheering each other on in one united group, instead of individual couples. Even the two groups of kids who had been hanging out at the walls before were in on the action.

"You're really good with them," Macie said.

Aaron looked out at the students that he normally saw in casual clothing, sitting in his classroom or walking in the halls, or messing around at lunch. "They're good kids."

Hemi, one of the linebackers from NHH's football team, was being spun around by the quarterback. Hemi was trying to act like he was graceful when he was anything but, and the crowd was laughing and cheering.

"Whoa!" He grabbed Macie around the waist with both hands and swung her to the side just as Hemi came barreling in their direction. He had barely gotten her out of the way before Hemi crashed into the refreshment table, sending the punch bowl to the ground, cookies and mints scattering in every direction. Hemi tried to stand up, but he slipped on the punch and fell back down. Students raced forward to pull him up, but they each ended up slipping and joining Hemi on the floor.

"Hold up," Aaron said, his arms out. "Let's get some towels over here before we have any more casualties." Then he turned to Hemi. "Are you okay?" When the boy nodded, he said, "How about the rest of you? Are we all good?"

When he got confirmations from everyone currently down on the ground, he turned to Macie. "Well, if this wasn't a memorable date before, it is now."

seven

MACIE

I t was easy to fake date Aaron. Macie found herself so naturally reaching for his hand as they walked around the room, or running her fingers along the back of his neck as they slow danced. If his students weren't convinced before that he was dating someone, they were now. It was too bad that he didn't want kids of his own because he was fantastic with them. As they had gone around from group to group, she could tell by the way he chatted with each of them that he truly cared about them and wanted the best for them.

After the janitor mopped up the punch, the dance quickly evolved from a dance into a party. Actually, it became more of a sport than a party once someone decided that it would be fun to play hockey with the fallen cookies, and it turned into one massive game with all the students and a couple of dozen cookie hockey pucks. For the first few moments, she, Aaron, and the other two chaperones tried to stop the game, but when they saw how much fun the students were having and the unifying effect it was having on them, they decided to join in.

The dance was ending in ten minutes, and although most of the students had left, Aaron had managed to arm a few kids with sweeper brooms, and they were turning cleaning up the mess into a game as well. The other chaperone couple had sunk into a couple of chairs along a wall. Aaron leaned against a wall at the end of the gym, facing the three boys who were cleaning up while simultaneously showing off to their dates. So far, their need to be impressive was working to get the gym back in order.

"I am exhausted," he said, running a hand down his face.

Macie practically fell against the wall facing Aaron, tiredness making any bit of gracefulness she had disappear. "Right there with you. How long was this dance? Like twelve hours?"

"It sure feels like it." Aaron stood up straight. "Wait. Was tonight a glimpse into what I can expect at your family party next Saturday?"

Macie laughed. "No, not at all." Then, once Aaron leaned against the wall again in relief, she added, "My parents mostly have carpet, so clean-up is a bit more hands-on," just to alarm him. And it worked. "No, I'm kidding; it won't be this crazy. Hopefully."

They both stood in silence for a moment, trying to recover enough strength to finish the last bit of clean-up, marshal the half dozen kids out to their cars, and lock the doors. For now, though, they were going to keep letting the kids work on clean-up.

Aaron grinned. "Tonight was fun."

"It was!" Macie said. "The most fun I've ever had at a high school dance, actually."

"Me, too." Aaron's face suddenly wasn't looking so tired. He was studying her, his expression soft, curious, thoughtful. "It was the most fun I've had on any kind of date in a long time."

Macie wondered if this was the most fun she'd had on a date in a long time, too, but she suddenly couldn't even think of a previous date she'd been on. All she could think of was tonight's, with Aaron. How rewarding it had been to banter with him and the students, how enjoyable it had been to let spontaneity take over when the dance hadn't gone as planned, how exhilarating it had been to dance with him while being cheered on by a crowd. To feel their way so seamlessly though a dance they'd never done before, yet somehow communicated to each other what to do without using words.

On the surface, she barely knew him. Yet a part of them had communicated on a level deeper than she'd been able to communicate with anyone in a very long time.

She had a list she'd made in her high school dating and relationships class of all the qualities she wanted in a future husband. As she got to know each person she dated, she put a mental checkmark next to each thing when the date exhibited that quality, or she'd mentally cross it out when they didn't. She put a check next to *Communicates with me well*.

"You're a fascinating woman, Macie." His eyes were searching her face, like he was trying to know more, to grasp clues about who she was.

Macie was just as eagerly searching his face. The more she got to know him, the more she wanted to know. She wanted to know it all. He reached out and placed his palm on her cheek, and she leaned into it, closing her eyes.

"Macie," Aaron said, and she opened her eyes as she stepped closer, closing the remaining distance between them.

His eyes dropped to her lips for a moment, which made her notice his lips. Lips that were soft and smooth and framed by the perfect amount of scruff. She met his eyes, and leaned in, her heels making her the perfect height, just as he leaned in.

And then just as her eyes were closing, she noticed his eyes flick to something behind her, and she remembered that they weren't alone. She whipped around to see all six

74

students who remained in the room all focused intently on the two of them, unmoving and silent, probably not wanting to break whatever spell had fallen over Macie and Aaron.

She sucked in a quick breath of air. She and Aaron had just come so close to *kissing*! What in the world had she been thinking? "Oh my goodness. I am so sorry." She turned to the left and then the right in quick succession, trying to remember what she was supposed to be doing right now.

"I'm sorry too. This wasn't part of the deal. I don't—"

"It was the formal wear," Macie said. "We can't be trusted in formal wear."

"It clouded our judgment," Aaron agreed. "That was a mistake."

Macie hurried to the wall that had the last row of chairs, and she grabbed one and folded it flat, then hung it on the rack. Aaron and the other couple joined her. *Come on, Macie!* she scolded herself. *For a second there you let hope sneak in, and that's exactly what you were stopping yourself from doing!*

This relationship, out of all the relationships she'd had over the past decade, was the one she could guarantee would never work. Everything here was for show. Maybe Aaron was trying to send the last few kids off with some fodder for rumors that would seal the deal, or maybe he was just as affected by the formal wear as she was— it didn't matter. There was nothing between them, and both of them knew it.

Having them both know that their relationship could go nowhere made the situation less awkward. Both of them knew that the other person wasn't going to have their feelings hurt that the kiss was stopped because neither of them had meant for it to happen.

When they finished and Aaron walked her out to her car, Macie said, "Mistaken almost-kiss aside, I had a very enjoyable time tonight."

"I did too." Aaron smiled. "So basically, all we have to do is stay away from formal wear, and we'll have smooth sailing from here on out."

She held out a fist and he bumped it with his. A kiss would've put the wrong cap on the evening. Their fist bump was a much better one, signaling what they were— teammates who had just worked together and successfully met a team goal and pulled off the next phase of their plan.

——

Macie slid into her seat on the fourth pew from the front of the chapel, her family taking up their customary three rows. As usual, she sat with her brother Everett, his wife Hannah, and their kids. Not only was Everett the brother nearest in age to her so they'd always been close, but he and Hannah also had four kids under the age of seven, and could use the help keeping them wrangled and somewhat reverent during the meeting.

Today, Macie held two-year-old Kristine on her lap as the toddler put baby Jesus in the manger of the activity book she held and folded the blankets over him.

The pastor finished his lesson on ways to keep Christ in Christmas, started talking about the importance of traditions— individually, as families, and as communities, and reminded everyone about the festivities going on in Nestled Hollow over the next week. As Macie listened, she noticed how contented she felt. Now that she wasn't going to worry about dating, she realized she was no longer holding one of Everett's kids in her lap, wondering and worrying about when she was going to be able to hold her own child in her lap. She just simply enjoyed being Kristine's aunt.

Her mom always said that she'd find her future spouse once she stopped stressing out about finding her future spouse, so maybe this plan was helping. She felt the hope creep in with that thought, and she squashed it quickly. She wasn't going to hope that this new plan was "working." That wasn't why she came up with the no-dating plan. She was just going to enjoy being Macie, without having to be *Macie: the woman in search of a husband.* Just Macie. That's all she had to be.

After the closing prayer, she helped her siblings and

their spouses and her parents carry, nudge, hold hands, or chase after all her nieces and nephews as they made their way with the rest of the congregation to the youth activity room for donuts, hot chocolate, and coffee. The room was a little too small for so many people, but a storm had blown in early that morning, and the first few flakes had started to fall just as she had entered the building. So the warmth and the happy chatter and the cup of hot chocolate in her hands felt right.

Several of the teenage girls had worn their Winter Formal dress to services today, and each of them gave her smiles like they were excited to be in on her secret. She chatted with them all and asked how their night was. She tried to think of a way to say "me dating your teacher isn't a secret! Shout it from the rooftops! That part's not the secret, so tell everyone!" in a subtle way, but apparently, it was too subtle, because the questions they asked were in hushed voices.

Normally, news in Nestled Hollow traveled fast. So many people had seen her and Aaron last night that she figured that everyone would be talking about it today. That didn't seem to be the case at all.

Like always happened in such a small space, the crowd moved around so much that she often found herself chatting with people who she might not have sought out on her own. Normally, that was one of the things she loved most about the months when it was too chilly to have the gathering outside.

At one point, she found herself chatting with a group of older women— Evia, Misty, and Margie. Apparently, Evia had a nephew, Misty had a grandson, and Margie had a friend with a son who were all perfect for her, and wouldn't it be simply marvelous if they set her up on a date? Maybe she could ring in the New Year with a boyfriend, because who wanted to start the New Year being alone? As gracefully as she could, she thanked them but said she was dating someone already, and then switched to a different group when an opening came up soon after.

Unfortunately, the next group she found herself in included Bo Charleston and Don Anderson. Normally she would've been relieved since the men usually didn't try to set her up on dates, but Don's son Paul was in town visiting. Shortly after Don introduced Paul, he said, "Paul, this is the woman I was telling you about. Don't you think she'd be just right for your friend Jake?"

Paul seemed just as uncomfortable with setting his friend up with a stranger as she was accepting a date with a stranger. She was so glad she had an excuse that wouldn't hurt Don's feelings or make Paul look any more uncomfortable than he already was. "You're always looking out for others, Don. Thank you for thinking of me, but I've already started dating someone seriously."

"Looks like we're a little too late, son. I knew I should've called you about this sooner!"

Macie and Paul shared a smile that told her he knew exactly what she was going through. Soon after, Don and his son Paul got pulled into a different group, and her little group was joined by Chad and Shelly Brown, the couple who owned the bakery on Main Street, and Ed and Linda Keetch. Her smile grew bigger at seeing their faces. She loved chatting with fellow Main Street Business Alliance members whenever she got the chance.

But after a few minutes of small talk, Chad said, "Shelly has an awesome little brother. Seriously, we love the guy. He's newly single, and I think you two would be great together."

"You would be. Do you want me to set you two up?"

Macie forced a smile on her face. "I've actually started dating someone." Her phone buzzed right then, so she excused herself, made her way to a corner, and pulled it out from her bag.

It was a text from Aaron.

> Aaron: Hey, there mysterious goddess. How's your Winter Formal hangover? I don't know about you, but I'm wishing I would've stretched before that dance.

Macie: Let's just say that I chose to wear flats to church today. I think my feet would've gone on strike if I wore so much as my one-inch heeled boots. Maybe our next fake date should be less physically taxing.

Aaron: Speaking of which...

Aaron: I have a group of friends—4 people, all married. They're cool and annoying and currently think I'm making you up. I showed up dateless to our last Wednesday Game Night, and I don't picture their razzing me will stop anytime soon.

Aaron: Will you come with me on Wednesday? I'm prepared to send many animated gifs of adorable animals and possibly toddlers begging if that will help convince you.

Macie: I have a better idea to convince me. This town is too full of too many helpful people who have no idea about things that happen at the high school. Be my date at a town event?

Aaron: Sold! Name the place and time, and I'm there.

Macie thought for a few moments. The pastor had just

mentioned everything going on this week, so it was all fresh on her mind. Which event would be best?

> Macie: The Main Street Business Alliance is in charge of a scavenger hunt on Tuesday. Meet me at Center and Main, 7:00. Macie: Dress warmly.

Macie smiled as she pressed send. The scavenger hunt was a perfect choice. Come Tuesday at about 7:30, everyone here would know she had someone in her life, and that she didn't need any interventions.

AARON

Aaron managed to find a parking space on Main Street. Sure, he'd only been on this street half a dozen times, and never during a town event, but it still surprised him that it was still so full of people. He got out of his car, pulled on his hat and then gloves, then adjusted his scarf and his coat. Each breath was making a cloud in front of him. How did they find so many people who were willing to brave this weather?

It was easy to see where the action was— a crowd of a few dozen people was assembling in the space where Center Street crossed Main Street, on the bridge that covered the creek that ran down the middle of the road. He made his way there, and saw Macie behind some long tables, standing next to her sister, chatting and smiling and organizing some kind of papers. A big Christmas bulb-shaped container sat on the table, with a small hole in the top. Macie reached in like she was swirling its contents around.

She was just as bundled up as he was, in her long coat, scarf, hat, and gloves, with her blond hair free and straight for the first time that he'd seen. It was too bad he couldn't date her for real because he wanted to more than he'd wanted to date anyone in a while.

But of all the women around, she was the most off-limits of them all. He knew she wasn't looking to date casually, and that was all he had to offer. Turning this into something more real wouldn't be fair to her. They were in this fake relationship as teammates, and teammates didn't do that to each other.

Macie looked up just then and she found him in the crowd almost instantly and her face brightened into a smile. He smiled back, and then their attention turned to a woman who was standing at a microphone.

"Hello," the woman said. "My name is Tory, and on behalf of the Main Street Business Alliance, I'd like to welcome you to the twenty-seventh annual Hayride of the Santas! Those of you who've been here before probably know the drill, but for those of you here for the first time and Sam— that's right, Sam, I saw you hop off the hay ride early last year—I'm here as your host and judge for the evening. We've got Cole here as your scribe and gift accepter, and Whitney and Eli as your documenters and additional judges.

"We've been coming to you asking for monetary donations for months, and I'm happy to report that we have enough money donated to help out a lot of kids this year who might otherwise wake up Christmas morning without any presents under their tree. You'll divide into teams of four or five people, so go ahead and get your teams together."

Aaron looked at Macie, and she motioned to him, then her, then her sister, and then pointed toward the end of the street. He turned and saw Macie's brother-in-law, the one he saw at With a Cherry on Top, walking in their direction. He nodded.

"Okay, *one* of you will come up to the table here, reach inside the giant ornament, and choose *one* piece of paper. On this paper will be the age and gender of the child who you will be purchasing a gift for. It will also list any preferences, colors, sizes, or things they might be currently interested in, along with a budget. Your goal is to brainstorm with your team about what to purchase for the child and to decide which Main Street store might have what you need. You'll go to that store, pick out a gift, and take it up to the register. The store will ring it up, attach the receipt to your paper, and sign off on it.

"You'll then bring the paper with the receipt stapled to

it, along with the gift, and check in with Cole. He'll verify that the present is appropriate for the age of the child and that you stayed within budget. You'll then wrap the gift *as a team*. Using only one hand each, and I expect no cheating here. Yeah, even from you, Frank. Your arm may be in a sling, but I've still seen you use those fingers on your injured arm for more things than I think your doctor ever intended."

The man who must be Frank laughed, holding up the arm in the sling, wiggling his fingers.

"Then you'll grab a new slip of paper from the ornament, and head off to find the second gift. The first team with five presents returned and wrapped wins!"

Everyone cheered. Aaron just chuckled. This town sure knew how to turn the typical sub for Santa into an event. He didn't pay attention to what kinds of city celebrations his own city did and suddenly wondered if they were anything like this.

"Here's the kicker, though. You can't run to the next store. We've got these two flatbed trucks filled with hay bales here." She motioned to one facing north on the road behind her and the other facing south on the road in front of her, and everyone turned to look. "You can only move from store to store on a hay ride, and May and George have been instructed that they can only move forward if everyone on board is singing a Christmas carol.

"Now I know what you're thinking. What if I'm right there at Wishstones Department Store, and I need to go next door to Toys 'n Trinkets? The buildings are practically touching! Can't I just slip next door? *No.* You can't go an inch past the edge of any store without being on a hay ride.

"So that means that yes, to go from Wishstones to Toys 'n Trinkets, you'll have to wait for the next hay ride to come along, sing carols while it goes down there to the end of Main, turns the corner, comes all the way along this side of Main, turns the corner again, and brings you back to almost where you started from. Sound like a blast? That's because it is! Okay, send your representatives up to get your first slips of paper, and then start brainstorming. You'll have about three minutes. When you hear the horn sound, the game is on!"

Macie waved Aaron up to the giant ornament, so he wove his way through the crowd and up to her.

"Well, hello, Dashing Man," she said as he reached his hand inside the ornament and grabbed a square of paper. "You're looking mighty fine all bundled up."

"So are you, Mysterious Goddess."

She grinned at him, and then motioned to her sister and said, "You remember my sister, Joselyn, right?"

"Good to see you again," he said as he reached out and shook her hand.

"Oh, and here's Marcus," she said.

He committed Marcus's name to memory and then shook his hand.

Marcus turned to Joselyn. "I checked with your parents, and Aria is doing great." He clapped his hands together. "Alright team, are we ready to win?"

Macie and Joselyn finished getting papers to each team, then Macie handed the ornament to Cole— the man who stood at the other table, who was going to be the scribe and present-wrapping official. Then the four of them huddled around the paper that Aaron held, and he read it out loud.

"So this child is a four-year-old boy, and we're looking for a toy with a forty-dollar budget. He likes dinosaurs and Legos and especially playing dinosaurs *with* Legos. His mom says he's a creative and determined kid."

"Toys 'n Trinkets," Macie, Joselyn, and Marcus all said at the same time.

"Toys 'n Trinkets it is then." The whistle blew, and Aaron pushed the paper into his pocket, slid his gloved hand into Macie's, and they raced to get on the back of the nearest truck. Aaron sat on a bale of hay, leaving room for Macie to sit next to him. She did, and leaned her head against his shoulder, snuggling into him for warmth. It felt nice having her so close. So he put his arm around her shoulders and held her tight to him so they'd both stay warm.

The twenty or so of them who seemed to be getting on the truck got on, but it didn't move. Macie seemed to be the first to realize why, and she jerked upright and sang,

"Dashing through the snow..." and the truck started to creep forward.

She sang so wonderfully off-key, it caught Aaron off guard. He wasn't exactly ashamed of his voice— he'd taken a year of choir back in high school to fulfill a music requirement and had learned a few things— but he wasn't proud of his voice, either. He usually shied away from singing out of embarrassment, but off-key or not, Macie was belting it out with such unabashed gusto that he couldn't help but want to join in. "In a one-horse open sleigh..."

Before long, all twenty of them were belting out the carol, and it was clear that Macie wasn't the only one who couldn't sing on key. Aaron found himself smiling as he sang. Why should people feel like they couldn't join in if they couldn't sing well? The cacophony was actually kind of nice, and in a way that didn't quite make sense, made him feel accepted.

As they neared Toys 'n Trinkets, they all perched on the side of the flatbed truck, and the moment it crossed into that store's territory, they leaped off and raced inside and to the Lego aisle.

Marcus grabbed a set of Lego Duplos. "How about these? They'll fit in our budget."

"I don't know," Macie said. "Those say they're for ages one to five, so he might grow out of them soon. We don't know how close to age five he is already. What about this kind? It says ages four to seven."

"The kid probably has chunky little hands," Marcus said, holding out his own chunky big hands as proof. "These will be easier for him to grab. Plus, if he wants to play Legos with dinosaurs, he probably wants to build something tall that a t-rex can come along and knock down. These kinds are the best for knocking down."

As the two of them debated the different sets, with Joselyn throwing in her opinion, Aaron picked up a set that was labeled for ages five through twelve. It said *Island Paradise* and had blocks that made palm trees and little huts whose doors could open and close, making it perfect for the smaller dinosaurs to get inside. He would've loved that set when he was a little kid.

"He isn't looking to knock down the blocks," Aaron said, his eyes on the set. "His mom said he's creative, so he wants to build a set the dinosaurs can interact with. And he's determined, so he likely won't be discouraged by smaller blocks." He held the set out to the others. "If we get him these, he can add to the set and keep using them for as many years as he'd like."

Macie beamed at him and looped her arm into his. Marcus took the set from Aaron, and looked at the front and then the back before giving a strong nod. "I think you're right. This is the one."

Further down the aisle, they found a bunch of plastic

dinosaurs that were inexpensive, so they grabbed a variety and raced up to the front. After getting their receipt and paper signed off, they hurried outside, but the truck had just passed their building. As they waited in the cold, rubbing their gloved hands together, Macie looked into the bag. "He's going to love these."

Aaron nodded. "This is a fun way to do it."

Marcus stepped behind Joselyn and wrapped his arms around her, kissing her on her temple. As the next truck made its way ever so slowly toward them, he wondered how many of the people were genuinely here for the kids, and how many were here for the free date.

Macie shivered and scooted closer to him. "There were a couple of Christmases when we were little where our parents didn't have money for presents, but it was okay because we had each other, and that was what mattered. But some of these kids don't have much of a home life. Can you imagine how sad it would be for them if they also didn't get any presents?"

When she said things like that, Aaron had a hard time picturing Macie as being anything other than genuine. Of course, before the very public shame of his parents' divorce had hit him, he had always thought they were genuine. Back then, he'd mistakenly thought Sabrina was, too, so now he didn't put much stock in his judgment. Aaron swallowed. "I can't imagine. That'd be awful." He squeezed Macie's hand. "Whoever this four-year-old is, he's going to love Christmas morning."

The truck finally made it to them, and the four of them hopped on, found seats on the hay, and immediately joined in singing *The Twelve Days of Christmas*. They only had to stay on for a moment before they jumped back off in the middle of Main Street, to the present wrapping station.

"Need a box?" a man asked.

"Yes!" Macie said. "I was imagining trying to wrap all these little dinosaurs with the four of us one-handed and thought that we'd made a terrible mistake. Eli, I'd like you to meet my boyfriend, Aaron."

She had hesitated for a moment before saying the word "boyfriend," and Aaron realized that it was the first time either of them had said it.

"Nice to meet you, Aaron," the man said as he shook his hand. "Here's your box and your wrapping paper and tape— each of you can choose which hand to put behind your back, but you can't switch once you've decided."

As it turned out, having four right-handed people all choosing their right hand made things more difficult than if they'd had a couple of less-skilled left hands in the mix. A woman with wavy auburn hair was taking pictures of their struggles.

"I think it's beautiful," Macie said when they were finished.

Aaron grabbed a bow with his right hand and held it while Macie pulled the plastic off the sticky part with her right hand, and he stuck it on top. "I'm not sure 'beautiful' is the word I'd use"—

"But it's done," Marcus said, "and that's what counts." He handed the present to Cole, and Cole checked it off the list and put it in a giant bin.

Joselyn raced to the table with the ornament and pulled out their next paper— an eight-year-old girl in need of pajamas, jeans, and socks— and they jumped on the next hay ride.

By the time they'd started shopping for the fifth paper they'd pulled out of the big ornament, it was clear it was down to just them and one other team to take the win. Aaron was pretty sure there wasn't an actual prize to be won, but both teams seemed very determined to win.

"I never would've guessed you were so competitive," Aaron said.

Macie shrugged. "Every year, it's my goal to win this. I've only succeeded once before, but I have a good feeling about tonight, especially with you as a teammate. You grew up swimming competitively, right?"

"I did."

"Were you any good?"

Aaron tried to hide a smile. Normally, he didn't like talking about that part of his life, but every once in a while when someone asked, the urge to tell them the truth about how good he was came on pretty strong. But the urge to know how someone felt about him when they didn't know always won out.

He shrugged. "I guess that depends on who you compared me to." That was *not* the answer he usually gave — that answer practically begged her to ask for details about who he'd be good compared to. And if he answered that, it might give her enough information to piece things together. So he shifted the focus ever so slightly. "And I love helping my team to win now. What do you say we win this?"

He could honestly say that he'd never shopped for all the ingredients for a Christmas dinner at a grocery store in two and a half minutes before, but they somehow pulled it off, got the receipt and had the cashier sign off their paper, then hauled all the groceries to the next hay ride.

As they hurriedly started singing *Deck the Halls*, like they would get there more quickly if they did, Joselyn pointed out that the other team had just jumped on their hay ride on the other side of Main, and it looked like they might both reach the present wrapping station in the middle at the same time.

"This is going to be difficult to wrap," Marcus said between fa la la's. "We'll have to be fast."

Macie stood up and moved to the back of the flatbed,

leaning out to look at something. Aaron got up and joined her.

She pointed back the way they'd just come. "There was a little kid in the alley between Best Dressed and the library. He was just crying. I think he's lost." She looked up and down the street, standing on her tiptoes to be able to see over the cab of the truck. "I don't see any parents nearby. We have to help him."

She moved to the edge of the truck, and Aaron grabbed the sleeve of her coat. "If we jump off, we'll be disqualified."

She met his eyes, hers pleading. "We *have* to. We're here to help kids in need—what's the point of it if we don't help a kid in need?"

He searched her eyes, trying to tell if that was what she really wanted, as a tear welled up in her eye. She batted it away, like it was a traitor ratting her out, and looked back toward the alley before meeting his gaze again.

"Let's go help him," he said as he wrapped his hand in hers, and they jumped off the back of the truck.

For the first time in the last decade, he trusted his judgment when he realized that Macie might just be the most genuine person he had ever met.

nine

MACIE

Aaron picked Macie up at her house, and together they made the drive to his friend's house in Mountain Springs. She studied him as they drove, and she could tell that something was different. He was quieter, and his eyebrows came together in the middle.

"Do you not want to go to this?"

"What? No. I love game night. My friends are good people."

Okay, not the answer she would've guessed, based on his face. She studied him some more. "Oh! You're nervous!"

Aaron looked confused and then chuckled softly. "I guess maybe I am." He thought for a moment, then said, "Are you nervous to have me meet your family on Saturday?"

"Totally. I'm always nervous when dates meet my family. I worry that my family might not like them, and worried that they'll scare him off."

"My family imploded when I was nineteen, and we all pretty much scattered at that point. But even before then, we weren't much of a family. We never willingly chose to hang out with each other. But these guys, they're my family. Their opinion matters to me a lot."

"And you're worried they might not like me?"

He glanced over at her. "How could they not like you?"

She shrugged. "Beats me. I'm the youngest, so I've been told my whole life that I'm adorable."

"They're going to love you. But if anyone is a tough crowd to convince, it's these guys."

―――――

Macie tried hard to remember everyone's names when Aaron introduced them, but she only managed to retain about half. After meeting everyone, though, the guys split off into the kitchen end of the open room, and the women gathered on the couches, and Macie was quick to pick up on and memorize their names. Ciara was the brunette who looked like a model, Timini was shorter, rounder, and constantly smiling, Annah was the quiet one who kept catching her off guard with her funny remarks, and Julie was the one who was seven and a half months pregnant who everyone was gathering around.

"So, other than the fact that I can't seem to hold on to anything," Julie said, "I think we're all ready for this baby to come! Of course, if I can't figure out the holding things part, I might need to hire a nanny just to keep me from dropping her."

"Oh, that goes away right after giving birth," Macie said. "Your joints have to loosen so your hips can adjust for birth, but it loosens all your joints, including the ones in your fingers. That's also why your feet are probably not fitting into your normal size of shoe."

It had seemed like a normal thing to say, but suddenly everyone was staring at her. "What?"

"How do you know that?" Timini asked in awe.

"I have six married siblings with kids. I became an aunt at fifteen. It kind of comes with the territory."

"Will you move in with us?" Julie blurted out, and everyone laughed. "No, seriously. We've got an extra bedroom up there and I don't have a clue in the world what I'm doing."

Macie knew the woman was joking, but it still made her feel good. Accepted. She looked toward the men and met eyes with Aaron. He gave her a smile and a nod like he was passing along his approval, too, and she smiled back.

"Wow, you two have fallen for each other *hard*, haven't you?" Ciara said.

For the smallest moment, Macie almost protested. Just because he kept proving that he was perfect over and over again didn't mean she was falling for him—she wasn't! Luckily, she caught herself quickly and kept up the show. "He is pretty fantastic."

Then it hit her— Ciara had said they had *both* fallen for each other. So they were already believing it; she and Aaron just needed to keep it up and his friends would be convinced.

Matt clapped his hands together. "Let's get this show on the road, ladies! If I have to stand next to this food much longer, I can't be held responsible for digging in early."

"Ooo, I can't wait to see what Aaron brought," Timini said.

"Aaron?" Macie asked. She knew he brought in a covered glass baking pan, but she honestly hadn't thought much about it.

"His food is divine!" Annah said. "I could hate you all and I'd still come just to eat Aaron's food."

So he could cook, too. Macie mentally checked off the *Must know how to cook* box on her *Future Husband* list. Then she chided herself for once again thinking of him that way. But how could she stop herself when he was standing there like that, holding his arm out to her with that brilliant smile and that *I care about you* face?

Instead of letting herself linger on the impossible, she focused her attention on the others. Like on the way that Ciara went up to Matt and they whispered something to each other, their noses touching, before she turned around and he wrapped his arms around her from behind and she snuggled into him.

Being here with all these happy couples was making her want, more than ever, what she didn't have. It always felt like everyone else got their happy endings. Why couldn't she?

Stop, she told herself. *Your perfect guy isn't even in your haystack, remember?*

———

After the food was cleaned up, and they all still sat around the table, Timini passed 3x5 cards out to all of them and said, "I can't wait to try this game out!"

Her husband rubbed his hands together in anticipation.

"Ian and I came up with this game last night and it's called...Oh my goodness, honey, we never came up with a name!"

Ian thought for a moment, and then blurted out "*Cloak and Dagger.*" Then, just a beat later, said, "*Duck and Cover.*

Oh, wait. No. I've got it. *Sneak Attack*. Come on, honey, we have to name it *Sneak Attack*."

"I can understand the 'sneak' part, but the other part isn't an attack. It's a challenge."

Ian spread his arms wide. "And what's an attack if not a challenge."

Timini sighed, and Ian put his hands together in a pleading motion, which worked on Timini, because she said, "Okay, this game is called *Sneak Attack*."

Shad reached out and gave Ian a fist bump.

"You've each got three green cards. Write on the top of each 'Attack.' On these cards, write down a different challenge on each. Something that one person could challenge any other person to do to see who wins. Like who can stand on one foot the longest, or who can make the other person crack a smile first. Something that will take about a minute or less to do. Everyone else decides who won the challenge, and whoever does wins the card."

"Now on your two yellow cards," Ian said, "write 'Sneak' at the top. Write down something that the person who gets that card will have to do without anyone else knowing that they're working on fulfilling a *Sneak* card. Like a phrase they have to say, or an action they have to do. You don't want to make it too easy, like scratching your nose or something, because it's everyone else's job to guess when they're doing something that's on their card. Because if you think you've caught someone else, you can yell," he glanced at his wife, then smiled, "'Sneak Attack!' and you'll win their card, but you can only call it if you weren't the one who wrote it. Get away with it, and you win the card. The person with the most cards at the end wins."

Macie's stomach was starting to feel queasy— probably from something she ate— but she willed herself to be okay, and started writing things on her card that she thought might be fun to do or funny to watch.

After they'd all turned in their cards and they were shuffled, Timini handed a yellow card out to each of them, and then one by one, they drew a green card and challenged someone to whatever it said. She laughed as Ian and Matt attempted to balance a pencil on their fingertip the longest while trying to blow the other's off, as Shad and Anna competed to see who could fake laugh the best, and as Julie and Timini attempted to whistle a note the longest.

All while watching for opportunities to do what her yellow card said: "Tell your spouse or date 'Baby, I'm never cold because you warm my heart.'" She had been faking this relationship for more than a week now. She could fake this line with no problem.

Aaron drew a card and read it out loud. "See who can run barefoot in the snow the longest."

Everyone's eyes darted to the patio doors and the snow

that covered the backyard just beyond them, worried that Aaron might challenge them to do it.

Aaron turned to Macie. "You wrote this one, didn't you?"

"Who, me?" Macie asked, trying to feign innocence.

"You did this with your siblings when you were little, didn't you?"

Macie chuckled. "Yes, and then we'd run back inside and wrap our feet in towels. How did you know it was me?"

"Because the only sane person who would do this is someone with enough siblings to talk her into it. So, Macie Zimmerman," Aaron said, slapping the card on the table between them, "I challenge you to a race barefooted through the snow."

They both took off their shoes and socks, rolled up their pants, and then made their way onto the patio with everyone else. Aaron grabbed her hand, they grinned at each other, and then he said, "Ready, set, go!"

Luckily it had snowed a bit just before they came, so there was a layer of soft powdery snow on top. Just under the top inch or so, though, the snow was a couple of days old, and with the sun shining on it during the day, it had made it icy and a little sharp. With each step, she landed on the soft cushion, and then broke through the crust from the layer just underneath, sinking into the snow up to mid-calf. Their feet pounded step after step, all the way to the end of the yard. And as they ran, she checked off her mental list, *Will do crazy, spontaneous things with me.*

They turned and raced back, still holding hands, and right before they reached the patio, Macie stopped in her tracks and dropped Aaron's hand. He didn't have time to react before his bare feet touched the snow-free patio. Apparently, he had forgotten it wasn't a race to the finish line— it was a challenge to see who could stay in the snow the longest. He remembered a moment too late, though, and hurried to step back into the snow.

"You might be Poseidon in the water, bro, but you're too late in the snow," Matt said as he clapped him on the back. "She's got you."

Poseidon in the water, huh? There was something he wasn't telling her. She made a mental note to ask him about it the next chance she got.

"I should've known better than to challenge the only experienced person here," he said as he placed a kiss on her forehead.

"You should've," she echoed as a pain shot through her stomach. She tried her best not to wince— not in front of people she was trying to impress. She shivered as she sat down in the kitchen and reached for her towel that Dennis held out, but Aaron grabbed it first and wrapped it around her feet. "You look so cold," he said.

She couldn't have planned the setup better. Two cards were going to be hers in a matter of moments. As she reached out and put her hand on his cheek, she said, "Baby, I'm never cold, because you warm my heart."

"Sneak Attack!" several people yelled at the same time.

Macie looked up, bewildered. "How did you know?" At least Shad, Annah, and Ciara had all called her out on it. Maybe even more of them that she didn't catch.

"Sweetie," Ciara said. "Don't ever become a used car salesman. You can't pull off a fake to save your life."

She met Aaron's eyes, and they shared a smile. There was something else in his smile, though, that she couldn't quite interpret. She didn't get a chance to figure it out before everyone was ushered back to the table.

Timini passed everyone their second yellow card. Because Matt was in her field of vision, she saw that he read his card, his eyes flashed at Aaron, and then he looked at her, and then back down at his card. He laid it face down on the table and said, "We've got to go."

Ciara had been laughing at something Annah had said, and she turned to Matt and said, "We do?"

Matt stood up, his chair legs scraping across the floor. "We do." He answered Ciara but kept his eyes on Aaron. Eyes that looked hurt and betrayed.

Aaron reached out and grabbed the card that Matt had left behind. Macie barely needed to lean in to see what the card said— it was one of the ones that she had written. *Say out loud "I lost my job today."* Macie's hand flew to her mouth as she realized what must have happened. What were the chances of her writing down something that was supposed to be difficult to pull off without being called out, and having it actually be true for someone? And then to have that person be the one who drew the card?

As Matt tucked in his chair and turned to leave, everyone at the table watching him in confusion, Aaron stood up, too, and slid the card into his pocket. He met Matt at the doorway to the entry, and the two had a whispered conversation, and at one point, Matt met Macie's eyes and then shook his head no to Aaron. Matt said something more to Aaron, and Aaron nodded his head several times, then clapped Matt on the shoulder before he and Ciara left.

Great. The group of people that Aaron was most concerned about impressing were these people, and Macie had totally messed it up. She couldn't tell how much of her sick feeling and the cold sweat breaking out on her forehead was coming from whatever she ate and how much was coming from how awful she felt about offending Aaron's best friend. He was probably wishing he had never brought her. Maybe he'd even want to take her home right away before she had a chance to inflict any more damage.

"Okay," Aaron said loudly as he came back to the table, taking in everyone's confused faces. "Matt wanted me to apologize that he realized he and Ciara needed to leave so quickly, and wanted me to make sure that we finish this round!"

The other three couples seemed to understand that they weren't going to get any more information about what just happened, and apparently respected Matt's wishes to act as if nothing happened. Everyone else refocused on the game with renewed vigor, like they were trying to make up for what negative thing just happened, but Macie couldn't. All she wanted to do was apologize profusely for what had happened. And then crawl into bed and pull the covers over her head.

As Aaron sat back down, he leaned in close and said, "I'm so sorry that happened. Are you okay?"

He was apologizing to *her*? Based on her experience dating men who had a tight group of friends, that wasn't what she was expecting at all. Even though she was now sure that the nausea that was creeping over her was very much sickness, she still smiled and felt the smile to her core. "I am, thank you for asking." And then she put a checkmark in her mental list next to *Shows that he puts me before his friends.*

Maybe she had been wrong all along. Maybe her perfect man was out there.

AARON

Aaron glanced up at the clock in his classroom to see how much time was left in class. He felt terrible that he hadn't noticed how sick Macie had been getting last night until she was so bad that he hadn't thought she'd make it the whole way back home without him having to pull off the side of the road.

Sure he'd been distracted by Matt thinking that he had betrayed a confidence and told Macie that he'd lost his job. Macie seemed to understand exactly what had happened and her role in it. So whenever she looked like she wasn't doing great, he thought it was because of that, and had just vowed to make the game more fun. All along, he should've been offering to take her home early instead.

He figured she'd be sleeping in to recover, so he waited

to text until his second-period class was watching a short documentary fifteen minutes before class got over.

> Aaron: How are you feeling? Don't answer if I just woke you up.

> Macie: Ha! No, I've been up for hours, sadly. Got a shop to run, animals to feed...

He sat up straighter.

> Aaron: Please tell me you're joking. You're sick! You've got an employee— Emily, right? Can't she take over?

> Macie: Not today. She can't come until 1:00.

> Aaron: What about family? Is there anyone who can help?

He glanced up at the clock. 10:20 on a Thursday morning probably wasn't the easiest time of day to rustle up help, but maybe there was someone free. He thought of how sick she had looked when he got her back to her house last night, and he couldn't believe she was doing anything other than being in a soft bed under a mountain of blankets.

Macie: Being the youngest in a big family means everyone thinks you need help and can't do things on your own. I've been fighting that for so long, I think I forgot how to ask.

Macie: Old habits die hard, I guess.

Macie: Or I don't know. Maybe I'm afraid to ask because they might start acting like I'm helpless again.

Macie: And I clearly shouldn't text when I'm so sick. It makes me philosophical and vulnerable.

Macie: Pretend I didn't send any of these.

Macie: Really, I'm doing great. I can make it until Emily gets here just fine.

Macie: Look! Puppies!

She sent a picture of three smaller dogs climbing on her as she sat next to one of her big dogs. Her face wasn't in the picture, but the fact that she was sitting on the floor and leaning against the wall wasn't a good sign.

Aaron: Nice use of animals. You got me with that distraction. Hang on, this video is almost over, and I'll need to talk to my students before they leave.

He discussed with his class some of the points the video made before the bell rang, and then excused them to go to their third-period classes. As soon as the last kid was out the door, he picked up the classroom phone and dialed the front office.

"Hi, Lisa, this is Aaron. I've got a prep period right now, and I just wanted to let you know that I'm going to run an errand and won't be back until closer to the end of lunch."

She thanked him for letting her know, and then he grabbed his coat, his cell phone, and his keys, and headed out the door, locking his classroom behind him.

An impressively short fifteen minutes later, he was at the doors of Paws and Relax with a grocery bag from Elsmore Market in one hand and the blanket he always kept in his trunk for emergencies in the other. He went inside and found Macie propped up in the corner where the big fish tank met the wall, a cat asleep on her lap, her black lab laying against one leg, a small dog in her arms, and another puppy pulling her sock off. Her face didn't have any color, and she looked miserable.

"Hi," he said.

"Aaron!" She pulled the little puppy out of her hair and back into her arms. "What are you doing here?"

He crouched down next to her and leaned over the dog to put his hand on her forehead. "I have officially ditched school, and I'm here until twelve-thirty to help out."

She looked around the room as if she was sure she'd see someone there that she'd missed. Like she didn't think he'd come if it weren't a date that was meant to convince some group of people that they were dating. "Why?"

He brushed the hair off her forehead. "Because even a fake boyfriend can be a good friend." Did he just willingly say something that would further entrench him in the friend zone when he very much hoped for more than that? He hadn't been able to stop thinking about her ever since the dance and he was starting to wonder if maybe, possibly, there could be something between them.

Except for every time he thought there might be, he remembered that she was just playing a part. Doing what she could to convince whoever they were around that they were dating.

But just then she looked at him like she wanted him to be something more, too.

It was probably just the sickness talking. Besides, he never wanted to get married, and she did.

"So do you think it was something you ate last night?"

She shook her head. "I wondered at first, but no. This

is definitely a bug. Hopefully only a twenty-four-hour one."

"What do you need help with?"

"I fed the dogs and cats already, but I haven't managed to get to the fish, hamsters, and geckos. And I've got a toddler group coming at eleven and I've got to get stuff taken care of by then."

She started to move like she was going to get up, but he put a hand on her arm and said, "Stop. That's what I'm here for. Just tell me where everything is."

She hesitated and then nodded. "The fish food is in that door—they need two pinches. The hamsters' food is in that cupboard right by their cage. Just fill their bowl to the top. And the geckos' food is next to the hamster food."

He stood up and raised the stuff in his arms. "Do you have an office or a back room where I can put this?"

"Just down the hall."

The office was the first room he found, and he set the grocery bag on her desk. The room was decently sized but didn't have a cot hiding behind the door as he had hoped. It did have some empty floor space, though, and she did have a blanket draped over the back of her chair, so he folded the blanket he brought in half and laid it on the floor. A glance around and he didn't see anything he could use as a pillow for her, so he took off his coat and folded it into a somewhat pillow shape, and put it on the blanket. Then he went back into the main room.

"Let's get you up," he said as he moved the animals off her.

"But my Parent, Preschooler, and a Puppy group will be here any minute."

He scooped her into his arms and stood up. "And those parents will appreciate it if you don't pass this bug along to their toddlers. I'm going to run the group, and you're going to get rest." He carried her into her office and lay her on the makeshift bed, adjusting the coat pillow. Then he grabbed the blanket off the back of her chair and spread it over her. Without the blanket hiding it, he noticed that her coat was on the arm of the chair, and spread that out on top of her, too, because she had a bit of a fever and figured she needed the warmth.

She snuggled into the blankets, shivering at first, and then relaxing. He stood up and started pulling things out of the grocery sack. "I brought you tissues; I'll put them right next to you here. And I got a pain reliever/fever reducer. Do you want one now?" Macie shook her head, so he put the bottle next to the tissues and set a water bottle next to it.

"For when you're feeling well enough to eat, I got you some chicken noodle soup from Elsmore's deli. I'll put it in your mini fridge. Do you need"— He had turned around to ask, but saw that she'd already fallen asleep. After adjusting the blanket to cover her shoulders more fully, he pressed his lips lightly to her temple and whispered, "Feel better," then he snuck out of the room and shut the door quietly behind him.

Parents and their preschoolers started coming into the shop before he even finished feeding the animals. He didn't have a clue as to how to run a Parent, Preschooler, and a Puppy event, but the parents gave him the gist of it and were mostly able to point out where things like balls and other dog toys were.

He made up games to play with the preschoolers and dogs as he went along and hoped that the group had fun and didn't feel cheated that Macie wasn't there. By the time the hour was over, he was ready to collapse himself. The cats had mostly left the room after sniffing everyone out, which left him with four parents, five preschoolers, two big dogs, and three little dogs, and he decided that they were way more exhausting than even his third-period Modern World History class. And that was saying something.

Once the place emptied of the kids and their parents and he got all the dog toys cleaned up, he opened the office door and peeked in. Macie was still sound asleep and looked so peaceful and less miserable than she had been that he couldn't bear to wake her up. He glanced down at his watch. There was no way he could find a sub this late, and it would only be thirty minutes before Emily came in anyway.

Then he remembered that Joselyn and Marcus worked just next door. He hurried into With a Cherry on Top, where thankfully they were both working and Joselyn was free enough to man the shop.

"Thank you," Aaron said as Joselyn walked into the shop, baby Aria in her arms. "I just didn't want to wake her."

"Thanks for looking out for her," Joselyn said. "I'll make sure she gets home and in bed once Emily gets here."

Aaron gave one last glance in the direction of Macie's office before he left. She had been so sick, he wondered if she'd even remember that he'd been there.

eleven

MACIE

Macie spent the day on Saturday at her parents' house, helping to prepare the food for the family Christmas Kickoff with her mom and oldest sister, Nicole, while other siblings helped out in other places. After putting the top crust on one pie, she wiped the flour off her hands and pulled out her phone for what was possibly the thousandth time, wanting to text Aaron, but holding herself back. She was dangerously close to falling for him, and if she just let herself text when she wanted to, she'd fall completely. For a guy who was only interested in being her fake boyfriend.

Falling for him would be dangerous. And dangerously easy. So instead of texting when she wanted to, she'd only texted once—on Friday, when she'd joined the land of the living again. Or at least the land of the semi-conscious.

She had thanked him for coming to rescue her on Thursday, and let him know that she was feeling much better and expected a full recovery by the party that night.

So she'd kept herself from texting, yet she'd still used the tissues he'd brought, taken his medicine, eaten his soup, and snuggled up to his coat that smelled like the most wonderful combination of cinnamon and pine with hints of chlorine.

And thought over and over about how thoughtful he'd been to show up when she most needed help, even when she'd told him that she'd be fine. And how it felt to have him carry her into her office. And how sweet it was that he took over her Parent, Preschooler, and a Puppy event. And how she could put a check next to *Takes care of me when I'm sick* on her list.

Come to think of it, texting probably would've been much less dangerous than thinking about him.

"Tell me about this new man in your life," her mom said as she put another filled pie on the counter in front of Macie.

Okay, Macie, she told herself. *Time to push the part of you that's seeing hearts for real out of the way, and pull out the part that is trying to convince everyone of the fake relationship.* The further this relationship went, the more difficult it was to switch into fake relationship mode.

"He's great, Mom," she said as she laid strips of pie

crust across an apple cranberry pie. "You're going to love him."

"Well, Joselyn has had nothing but good to say about him. I'm glad you're finally bringing him to meet us."

"They haven't even been dating for two weeks yet, Mom," Nicole said as she rolled out a pie crust. "Janet, Mindy, Masen, and Chris, freeze right where you are!" Macie's attention flew to the back doors where Nicole's four kids had just burst into the house. "Get those snowy boots and coats off and hung up before you track it through Grandma's and Grandpa's house! I heard he brought you soup. I tell you, if a man brings you soup when you're sick, he's a keeper."

"Kennon, Zach, and I have the lights all finished!" her dad called from the far side of the family room. "Can I ring the bell yet?"

"Five minutes, Dad," Joselyn said from where she and their sisters-in-law, Audra and Lia, were helping her to set the long dining tables that separated the kitchen from the family room. "Just let us finish with the tables before you add to the," she stepped over Brindley, her parents' dog, and then over Katie, her three-year-old niece who was chasing her, "crazy."

The doorbell rang just then, and everyone's heads jerked up, all knowing that the only person who was coming who wouldn't have just walked in was Aaron.

"I'll get it," Macie said, taking off her apron, brushing

the flour from her hands on a towel, and heading toward the front door. Her mom did the same. She had a suspicion that her dad was on his way from the other end of the hall, too.

She opened the door, and Aaron stood on the porch, looking tall and lean and perfect and covered in snow and holding a vase of Christmas-themed flowers.

"Oh, wow. It's really coming down out there, isn't it?" Macie helped to brush the snow off his coat and scarf, and then he stomped his feet and stepped inside.

"You look beautiful," he said. "The flour on your cheek is a nice touch." He reached a hand out and brushed the flour off her face with his knuckles. "How are you feeling? You look about three hundred times better than when I last saw you."

"I'm feeling all the way better. Thank you. And thank you for Thursday."

He smiled, then his eyes shifted behind her, and she turned to see that it wasn't just her parents who were crowded around the back of the entry, but at least half of her siblings and their spouses. "Aaron, I'd like you to meet my parents, Emeline and Joseph."

"Thank you for inviting me to your home," Aaron said as he handed the flowers to her mom. "It's so nice to meet you."

Her mom accepted the flowers and gave him a one-armed hug and said, "We're so pleased you could come. We've heard nothing but good things about you."

Then he shook her dad's hand, and her dad added, "Don't do anything to hurt my little girl, and you're always welcome here."

Macie held an upturned hand toward everyone else in the room, and said, "Well, I'd like to say that I'll introduce you to everyone else, but we both know this isn't even close to everyone else. Here, let me take your coat."

As they walked into the kitchen from the hall at the right, she thought about how proud of herself she was for not dwelling on how sweet it was that he brought flowers for her mom. Instead, she leaned in and whispered, "Nice touch with the flowers," and offered her fist. He bumped it with his.

When they reached the great room, her mom placed the flowers from Aaron in the middle of the dining tables and took a step back. "There. Now everything is perfect."

"So does this mean I can ring the bell?" her dad asked.

"Yes, dear, you can ring the bell."

Her dad went on to the back patio and rang the big bell he had attached to the patio roof like he was calling the ranch hands in for the midday meal. He'd installed it clear back when she was a sophomore in high school and her oldest brother Oliver had just finished building his house. Twelve years later, it still brought him just as much joy to ring it to call everyone home.

Within minutes, the patio was swarming with family, brushing the snow off their coats and hats and gloves and stomping their feet, before pouring into the house and removing winter gear. A lot of the coats and scarves made it onto the hooks, and some boots were paired and standing upright along the wall, and the rest was in one massive pile.

His dad's face was beaming as all the kids gathered around him and the Christmas tree. Like always, it was a live tree that he went into the mountains to chop down, and by the looks of it, was nearly ten feet tall. Ladders of various sizes were placed around the tree.

"Who's ready to decorate this tree?" The kids cheered loudly, then he said, "Remember, you've got to be eight to get on the taller ladders, and five to get on the shorter ones, okay? Raise your hand if you are one, two, three, or four." All the littlest kids raised their hands. "You all get something even better than a ladder. If there's ever an ornament you want to put up high, you've got me. I'll be just like a ladder on a fire truck and lift you as high as you need. Okay, you all know what to do— let's get this tree decorated!"

"It looks like your dad loves this," Aaron said.

"He really does."

"Do you want to give me everyone's names?"

Marcus, who was standing nearby, said, "Don't do it. There are too many— they'll all just swirl into a fog. It took me months to learn all of them. I still forget some sometimes."

"He does not," Joselyn said. "Don't let him fool you. He even has their birthdays memorized."

"Well, there's a lot of competition here for favorite uncle! I have to do what I can to stay ahead of the game." He crouched down, and as four-year-old Brighton ran past to grab another ornament, he said, "Who's your favorite uncle, buddy?"

"You are!" Brighton said and gave him a high five with an impressive amount of force behind it.

"I want to hear them," Aaron said.

"Really?" Macie searched his face, to see if she could tell if he wanted to know, or if he was just trying to play the part of the perfect boyfriend. How had she once thought this fake relationship was a brilliant idea? She hated never being able to tell how he really felt. "Okay, well that's my oldest brother Oliver over there on the couch next to his wife Audra. That's Larissa, Riley, Claire, Sophie, and that was Brighton. Then there's Zach with Cameron in his arms, his wife Lia is over there, and Trevor and Katie."

She looked at him to see if he was overwhelmed already, but he motioned for her to keep going. "Then my sister Nicole and her husband Noble are there, and they've got Janet, Mindy, Mason, and Chris. My brother Kennon is with his wife Rosabella there, and their sons are the ones at the tops of the ladders— Brian and Brandon. Everett is over there, and his wife Hannah is holding Madison. She's my youngest niece; she's only two months old. They've got Drew and Jason there, and Kristine is over— Kristine! No eating the dog's tail! And then you already know Joselyn and Marcus and Aria."

Aaron smiled as he watched the kids decorate the tree, and that made Macie smile. She had worried that being around such a big family might be too much for him, especially since his was small and didn't include kids. But if she had to guess, she'd say that he was enjoying himself.

Of course, he had proven himself to be a pretty good faker.

When it was time to eat dinner— their traditional prime rib, roasted Brussels sprouts, rosemary roasted baby potatoes, and a big range of salads made by each of her siblings— Aaron was gracious and kind and started conversations with everyone. He even made sure the kids weren't ignored. In fact, beyond not being ignored, he had a gift of making each of them feel important and special. Back when she was sixteen, she hadn't even known to put that on her list. She had just put an all-inclusive *Would make a good dad* on it. But this kind of thing was exactly what she had meant. She put a bunch of checkmarks next to that on her mental list.

"Who made this butternut squash and apple casserole?" Aaron asked the table in general.

"I did," her older brother Oliver answered.

"This is one of the best things I've ever tasted," Aaron said. "We need to talk after."

Oliver nodded back, and she could see in Oliver's eyes that he liked Aaron and accepted him. *Oliver.* Her brother who was the harshest judge of her boyfriends out of everyone. She tried to remember if he had ever had that look in his eyes when seeing anyone she had dated.

Maybe she didn't need a break from dating. Maybe she just needed a break from dating all the wrong people. Maybe the right guy was sitting next to her.

When the meal was finished and cleaned up, her parents gathered everyone into the family room, and they all found spots on the floor facing the fireplace.

"It's time for the annual hanging of the stockings!" her mom said, her hands clasped in front of her.

It had always been one of Macie's favorite parts of Christmas. She wondered what Aaron would think of it. Her mom pulled out the pile of stockings that were all linked together. With her own stocking in one hand, her mom handed her dad's stocking to him. They each pulled on their end, and everyone's stockings unfurled. Macie and all of her siblings' stockings were connected between her mom's stocking and her dad's, one after another, a row of nine stockings, each linked to the next with gold rings. Each of her siblings had their spouse's stocking linked to theirs, and each of their kids was linked to the two of them, hanging down in a line before it connected with the next family's.

Each of her parents used big clamps to fix their stockings nice and sturdy to the mantle, everyone's stockings hanging between them.

"We've got three new stockings to add this year," her mom said and pulled the stockings from the box. "We've got Cameron's since he was born just the day after Christmas last year." She held the stocking out and everyone *Ooh*-ed an *Ahh*-ed.

Macie leaned into Aaron and whispered "My mom makes every stocking, and they're all different. You've got to see them up close."

"And then we've got Aria's," she said as she held hers up, "and of course baby Madison's."

Her parents used the golden rings to link each of the three new stockings to the bottom of each of their families and then linked them to the next family. Then her dad took a step forward to tell the annual Christmas Link story.

"As you can see, you are linked to everyone else in our family up here. All those links, connecting us, are what make us strong. Happy. Loved. United. Every single person represented here is an important link in our family. You are important. You matter. You are loved by all the family surrounding you today. Nothing will ever change that. There is nothing that you can ever do that will change that fact, not even death."

Macie's mom reached out and touched the stocking with Cambry's name that was linked right below Zach's and Lia's stocking.

"We love you. You matter. Your relationships with your family matter. So when disagreements or misunderstandings or hurt feelings happen—and they will, we're all human—talk it out. Fix it. Nurture each other extra in those moments. Keeping those relationships takes work. But it's some of the most valuable work you can do. You matter. The people around you matter. Family matters. Those relationships matter. Keep working on them, and keep looking out for every chance you can get to serve each other because that's what keeps those links strong."

Two years ago, Joselyn's stocking was just like Macie's —linked together yet hanging alone. And then last Christmas, Joselyn's had Marcus's stocking linked next to it. Now they had a stocking hanging below them.

Seeing her family's stockings all linked together always made Macie feel like she belonged and was valued. But she wanted more. She wanted her own stocking links to go down, too, just like all of her siblings' stockings did. She had wanted it for years but never had the longing hit her as strongly as it was right now.

She snuck a glance at Aaron and could tell by the way

he was staring at the stockings and blinking faster than normal that what her dad had said had touched him too. He wrapped his arm around her shoulders.

"What do you say we work on making those links even stronger? Who's ready for their Secret Service names?"

All the kids cheered and jumped up from where they were sitting on the floor. They each came up to Macie's mom and pulled a name out of the bowl she was holding, the littler ones racing to their parents to have them read the name and tell them who they'd be doing secret acts of service for. Macie's dad brought around the bowl that had her siblings' and their spouses' names in it and had each person pull a name out. Macie pulled one out and looked at Aaron, but his eyes were still fixed on the stockings.

AARON

Aaron had to admit that the tree lighting was pretty cool. You could hardly even tell that all the ornaments were clumped in clusters on the bottom half or up in lines along the edges of each ladder.

He hardly had time to admire it, though, before Macie's brother Zach leaped out of his seat and said, "Who thinks they can outlast me? I'm planning to make it around the playground."

Zach kicked off his shoes and started pulling off his socks, and Aaron's eyes grew wide. His attention flew to Macie. "When I asked if you ran outside barefoot in the snow with your siblings when you were little"—

Macie ducked into a shrug. "Yeah, I didn't quite mention that it wasn't *only* when we were little. What? It's not like we do it all the time. Just during Christmas

Kickoff. So..." She looked to the left and the right. "Do you want to see if we can outlast Zach? He's tough."

Aaron laughed. One thing was for certain, life with Macie would never be boring.

Did he just imagine his life with Macie? It had been a very long time since he'd done that with anyone. He looked at her for a long moment, admiring how her curls cascaded down her shoulders, the way her smile lit up her entire face, the way she got excited about the little things. Not to mention the way she looked in that red sweater and jeans. "Sure. We survived last time, after all. And I don't have to worry about you getting too cold, because I warm your heart, baby."

"You better believe it," she said, putting her hand on his chest and sending heat zinging to it.

"I'll grab the towels," Macie's mom said as he and Macie took off their shoes and socks and rolled up their pant legs.

Aaron was surprised— most of the adults were taking their shoes off, along with all the older kids. Of course, it was a family event with the Zimmermans. He should have guessed. They all raced out to the covered patio, braced for the cold, and came to an abrupt halt. Snow covered everything so deeply, it was difficult to make out what any of the bumps were.

"When did it snow this much?" one of Macie's sisters-in-law asked.

"Look at how much it's still coming down, too," Nicole said. "The forecast said it would only be a couple of inches!"

Macie gazed across the lawn, a look of wonder and disbelief on her face. "This has to be up above our knees."

"Well," Zach said, "I guess we'll be swimming to the playground then." He dove off the patio into the snow, like he was diving into water to swim laps.

"Zach!" his wife yelled. "You're going to be frozen down to your bones!"

"Especially if I can't figure out how to swim any faster than this," he said as he made motions that mimicked freestyle, but didn't make him move forward at all.

They all made their way back into the house, including Zach, whose wife made him brush all the snow off him before entering. Macie's oldest brother pulled his phone out of his pocket and furrowed his brow at the screen. Then another brother pulled his out. Aaron had felt a ding from his about the same time, so he pulled his out, too.

ALERT: HEAVY SNOWFALL AND
AVALANCHE WARNING IN THE CLEAR
CREEK AREA; I-70 IS CLOSED FROM
MOUNTAIN SPRINGS TO COPPER
MOUNTAIN.

"Oh. I guess I need to...Oh."

All around, everyone pulled out their phones and showed them to the people nearest them. Aaron just kept staring at his, trying to make his head work through the implications, then he hurried into their living room and looked out the front window at his car. It was covered so deeply in snow that he could barely tell what color it was anymore. And with the roads closed, he wasn't going to be going home. "I guess I should probably go before I can no longer find my car and see if I can get a room at the hotel."

"Nonsense, son," Joseph said. "We've got a guest room right here you can use. Even if we got your car unburied, you wouldn't make it two feet until they plow these roads."

"Of course, we'll put you up here," Emeline added. "I'll go get the bed made up."

As they walked back toward the family room and kitchen, one of the older kids said, "With this much snow, Grandma, I don't think we'll be able to make it home either. It's probably deeper than Brighton! If we go home, we'll lose him in the snow and he'll be gone forever. I think we're all snowed in, and our only option is to have a giant sleepover like we do on Christmas Eve."

"The boy has a point," Macie's dad said.

Before Aaron knew it, it was no longer just him sleeping at Macie's parents'. It was everyone. All thirty-five of them, all sleeping at the same house.

"You know the rules," Emeline called out. "Mine and Grandpa's bedroom is off limits, and so is the guest room. Anywhere else is free game."

"But not the bathtub," Larissa said, giving Brian a pointed look.

"Oh, don't worry, I learned my lesson last year when I had to get up and leave every time someone had to go to the bathroom in the middle of the night."

As Aaron and Macie helped all the kids get their beds set up in all corners of the house, Aaron thought about all he'd witnessed this crazy, unexpected night. He'd never known a family like this in his life. His parents had always said that family was important, and they supported his swimming and Aliza's dancing every step of the way, right up until the end.

But they never cared about each other the way that this family did. Strangely, Joseph's talk about the family and the links that connect them made him miss Aliza. His parents, even. He called them every six months or so, and visited occasionally, but usually out of a sense of obligation. Missing them was new.

Some of his friends were closer to their families than he was with his, but none of them had families that were anywhere close to this either. He didn't even hear people talk about families like this. It had to be a show. A front that Macie's parents were putting on, just like the front his parents put on. Like his ex-fiancée had.

But even so, as he and Macie worked side-by-side, he couldn't deny the attraction he felt toward her. She was one of the few people he had ever met who looked just as beautiful when she was working through the flu as she was in a ball gown. And as much as he wanted to reach a hand out and run his fingertips along her cheek and neck, it was more than just her looks. He was drawn to her because of everything she did. Because of everything she was.

When they finished with the beds, and a group of nieces and nephews started climbing on Macie to have her read them a story, he excused himself to go get his bed set up, since he'd stopped Macie's mom from doing it.

As he worked, he realized how much his heart was getting tied up in this. Just like it did back with Sabrina when he was twenty. And if he ever needed a reminder of how painfully that turned out, all he had to do was Google his name. He couldn't invest his heart in something again that could turn out to be just a front. And there was no way a family like this wasn't.

He walked out of the guest room and paused. Macie's parents were right across the hall, standing in the doorway of their darkened room— the one place they thought they had to themselves, their back to him and oblivious of his presence.

"Every time I think I can't love you more," Emeline said, "I look at this family we created together and the way you love them, and my heart just bursts."

"Forty-one years," Joseph said. "Forty-one years and my heart still leaps every time I see you. Life has been heaven on earth with you in it, my dear Emeline."

Aaron stepped back into the guest room, stunned at what he just witnessed. They weren't putting on a show for their kids or anyone else. They were completely alone, and that was how they spoke to each other when they thought no one was looking.

It was all true then?

Everything he witnessed in this family tonight. It was real? Genuine? The last time he truly believed that love like that was possible, he was just a kid.

Now he understood what Macie wanted. He finally grasped why she was searching so hard to find the perfect spouse. She wanted this— a marriage like her parents had. And he finally learned why. This was what he wanted too. Deep down inside, it was what he had always wanted; he had just never known it before now.

When he got back to the family room, Macie and a couple of her siblings were tucking the last few kids into bed. She looked up at him and smiled, then stepped over the sleeping bodies and made her way toward him as her siblings went to other rooms, probably to check on other kids.

As she neared, he whispered, "You're even graceful when you're stepping over sleeping kids."

"You haven't seen me trying to do the same thing after being woken in the middle of the night to ward off monsters when a kid needs to go to the bathroom."

"True." The moonlight bounced off the snow, making

outside unusually bright for eleven p.m. The moonlight spilled through the kitchen window and lit up the side of Macie's face. This entire night, something inside him had been building and building— a connection to the heart of Macie that pulled him to her. He reached out and put a hand on her cheek, needing to feel its silkiness against his skin, and she responded by putting her hand on his chest. He closed his eyes as the electricity from his whole body rushed to meet her hand.

Snow fell cold and beautiful just outside the window, but Macie stepped close enough that he could feel her warm breath against his neck. It wasn't just him who felt the connection, then. It was as if the two of them were forces being drawn together by something unconcerned about whatever protests they had.

And maybe nothing else beyond showing Macie how much he cared about her did matter. He moved his hands to her waist, and she brought her second hand up next to the first on his chest. Her eyes shifted to his lips, and suddenly her lips were all that he could focus on as the snow fell all around them.

Macie leaned into him, a hand slipping up to the back of his neck, her fingers in his hair, and he brought his lips to hers. Her lips were soft and moving on his carefully, testing to see if this was okay. He responded, his kisses being just as careful and questioning.

After a few moments, her second hand flew to the

back of his neck, and she pulled him in closer. He pulled her in tight and kissed her with an urgency that matched hers, pouring everything into it that he had felt not only in the past few hours but since the day he'd met her.

Macie broke contact first and whispered, "Wow."

Aaron tried to steady his ragged breathing enough to whisper back. But before he did, he heard, "Smoochie smoochie! *Mwah, mwah, mwah.*" And then more kissing sounds followed by a whole lot of giggling.

"Trevor! And Janet, Mindy, and Sophie! You all are supposed to be sleeping!"

"But we're not," Janet said, "and we caught the whole show."

"I'm not asleep either," three-year-old Katie said.

Aaron felt heat rushing to the back of his neck, and Macie's blush was visible in the moonlight. She motioned to them and then the general vicinity of his room and then somewhere else, like she wasn't quite sure where to direct her focus, then said, "We better, um—"

"Yeah, we should," Aaron agreed, and they both went off to their separate parts of the house.

thirteen

MACIE

Macie was in her office, studying spreadsheets and brainstorming when the bell at the front door chimed. Reese and Lola, who had been lying at her feet, jumped up and ran to the main room. School wasn't out yet, and she didn't have any events planned, which meant it was a walk-in customer. Those were some of her favorites! Sometimes she got tourists or just stressed-out adults who needed a mid-workday boost. Since she'd been spending more on advertising, it was happening more and more frequently.

She walked out to the main room and saw her dad crouched down next to her dogs, trying to give them both equal attention when both wanted his undivided attention.

"Dad!" she said as she hurried forward and hugged

him. "This is a nice surprise. What are you doing around here in the middle of the day?"

"I just needed to stop by home and change clothes before heading to a business meeting in Denver. I thought I'd drop in and see how my favorite youngest daughter was doing."

They sat down in two of the chairs along the wall. "I'm doing great, Daddy."

"That Aaron sure seems like a nice boy."

"He really is," Macie said, thinking back to the Christmas Kickoff party, their kiss in the kitchen, and the family breakfast the next morning before he headed back home.

"You make sure he knows he's welcome anytime, okay?"

"I'm pretty sure he got that message by the sendoff you and Mom gave him yesterday morning."

He reached out and squeezed her hand. "Alright, alright. I'll stop trying to nudge the relationship and just let it play out on its own. Now tell me, how's the decision on whether or not to buy this building coming along?"

Macie took a big breath, and then let it out in a fast huff. "I don't know, Dad. As I've been pushing to grow the business more, the numbers have been coming in where I was hoping they would. Not that one month's worth of data is enough to base a decision on. There are just so many variables."

"So the numbers are coming in good, but..." he prodded.

"But getting sick scared me. If Aaron hadn't stopped in to help, I don't know what I would've done. I was trying to convince myself that I could just push through it and everything would work out, but Dad, I was really sick. Too sick to have done what he did, no matter how hard I tried or wanted it.

"I know I was only sick for a couple of days. But the truth is, if I'm ever out of commission, even for a little while, this business is, too. It relies too heavily on me being one hundred percent." It was a fear that she hadn't voiced before, and now that she said it, she felt it even more strongly.

"Can you get another employee? Then you'd have enough overlap that if any one of you was sick or hurt or what have you, there would always be someone to cover for you."

Macie shook her head. "I can't and still have the numbers be where they'd need to be to buy the building."

"Is there more growth potential? If so, maybe you could move forward knowing that things would work out."

"I don't know. That's impossible to tell without more market research and testing. And those things take time."

"Would you like me to take a look at your books with you, maybe see if there's something you're missing?"

"That's okay, Dad. You've got a meeting you need to get to. I'll get this figured out."

"I know you will. You're a bright, determined girl who knows how to use that business degree you've got. Just know that the offer stands anytime you want it." He rubbed Lola's head and ran his fingers back and forth behind Reese's ears, just like they liked it, then pet the two dogs and one cat that had sidled up to him, then left.

Macie headed back to her office to work her way through another scenario. The more she thought and planned and figured things out, the more things popped into her head that she would need to account for. And the more she got worried about committing to something so big.

Eventually, Emily came into work, and things got much busier out front. Still, she worked through plan after plan. But all the playing and laughing going on in the other room was distracting, and she found herself spending more and more time glancing over at the coat Aaron had left cradling her head when he'd lain her down on the makeshift bed he'd made for her on the floor last Thursday.

She'd taken the coat home with her, and had meant to bring it to the Christmas party to return it to him, but she'd forgotten. She still wasn't ready to analyze her forgetfulness to see if it had been strictly on accident, or if a part of her wanted to keep it a little while longer just to feel him near. Or to give her an excuse to go see him.

Whatever the reason behind it was, she did have the coat, and she did need to return it to him. She glanced up at the clock. School was out, but he'd probably still be there. She put on her coat, grabbed her purse, and slung his coat over her arm.

———

The front office let her know that he had swim team practice today that was probably just about over, so she headed toward the end of the school with the gyms and the indoor pool. When she went through the doors, his entire team was out of the water, pressing their towels against their suits and hair as they listened to him give details about when their next practice and meet was. A chlorinated humidity hung in the air, so she immediately set his coat on a bench, removed hers, and laid it on top of his. Aaron dismissed them all to the locker rooms.

Macie figured that he would probably turn around and walk in her direction, but he didn't. He pulled his shirt off, tossed it on the benches along the sides, and dove into the pool. She didn't mean to just stand there, watching him when he didn't even know she was there. But his strokes as he glided through the water were just so... beautiful.

He swam freestyle, one arm at a time coming up out of

the water, then sinking back in with such powerful force and perfect rhythm, his head turning to take a breath every fourth stroke. His legs kicked so strong and lean and every line and angle of every movement was breathtaking. Each turn at the ends of the pool was flawless, not a wasted motion, not a muscle out of line.

Watching him was mesmerizing, and gave her the strangest sense of déjà vu. Then he switched to swimming the butterfly stroke, his arms coming out of the water at the same time, those powerful legs kicking together.

The third time his arms came out of the water, she gasped.

This wasn't the first time she'd seen him swim. It had been a long time since she had, but she immediately knew it was true. The more she watched him swim, the more details came back to her. The pool. The crowds. The suit, the swim cap, the diving blocks, the judges, all on her family's TV. She had been what? A senior in high school? No, not quite. It was the summer Olympics, right between her junior and senior years. And he had been the golden child of the USA Olympic Swim Team, swimming in several individual and team events.

How had she not recognized the name? Probably because it was just normal enough to not stand out. There was something people used to chant. She racked her brain trying to remember.

"Aaron Hall," she whispered the chant. "Take gold in all."

Something happened, though. The details just hadn't been in her head enough. Like she hadn't seen it happen herself; she'd only heard about it, so it didn't stick.

He swam up to the end of the pool nearest Macie, touching the side of the pool with both hands at the same time. Then he stood and brushed the hair out of his face. The moment he noticed her standing there, his face broke into a smile. He must've been able to read the expression on her face, though, because the smile fell right along with his shoulders. She could tell that he suspected she knew.

Yet still, he put on a smile and acted as if nothing happened. "You're a nice surprise. What brings you to the chlorine-scented, humidity-filled part of town?"

"Aaron, you are an Olympian! A gold medal-winning Olympian!"

He didn't respond— he just glanced at the lane beside him, like he was wishing he'd kept on swimming.

"Aaron, why would you not mention that? Why would you not tattoo it on your arm or print it on all your t-shirts?"

He took a long breath, then put his hands on the side of the pool and pushed himself out. He walked toward her, the pool water running down his chest, arms, and legs, accentuating muscles that she had only felt a hint of when she'd put her hand on his chest. Then he turned, grabbed a towel from the rack, pulled it down his face, then dried off his neck. "Because I don't have the best of memories associated with the Olympics."

Macie's brows crinkled and her head cocked to the side as she tried to remember what had happened. He blew out a breath. "Okay. I'll tell you the story— I'd rather you didn't find it out by Googling it. Give me ten minutes to shower and change."

She sat down on a bench to wait and had to repeatedly stop her fingers from inching toward her cell phone, where the internet was waiting, ready to give her answers. But no— she respected Aaron and could wait to hear them from him.

As long as he hurried.

Her cell phone was so close, though. *No, Macie,* she told herself. *You can wait.*

When he came back into the pool room, he was dressed in slacks and a button-down shirt. She grabbed the coats and he led her out of the pool, through the gyms, and into the atrium, an octagonal room with tall windows on six sides. They sat on one of the couches that she'd curled up on to study plenty of times back in high school.

"Okay," Aaron said, "tell me what you already know."

"I know that you were young. Now that I'm doing the math, nineteen." He nodded, so she continued. "And you were supposed to swim in a lot of different races."

"Five."

"And you were a gold hopeful in several of them."

"Three."

"And you won gold in some..."

"Two gold, one bronze."

"But then something happened, and you didn't compete in your last event. I can't remember what."

"My parents happened. I didn't know it at the time, but they'd been having disagreements for years over the money all the coaching and traveling to national meets cost, versus the endorsement deals I'd eventually get by being an Olympian, over which one of them was doing it so they could have a trophy family and the bragging rights that came with it, and which one was doing it with my best interests in mind and just wanted to set me up for a successful future.

"And since their private marriage had 'ended' years ago, which one of them was flaunting extramarital affairs in the other's face the most."

"Oh, Aaron."

"My parent's public marriage had been pretty close to perfect, even from my point of view. I got my first endorsement offer between races, and it blew the lid off an argument that had been brewing between my parents for years. They had hidden every fight they'd ever had from me and my sister Aliza and the rest of the world. That final explosion, though, happened right in front of me.

And Aliza. And everyone else in the press room. Moments before my final race."

He was quiet for a few moments, his fingers flipping the zipper pull from her coat that was lying on his leg back and forth, back and forth.

"I was at the Olympics, I'd had three medals hung around my neck, and had received my first endorsement offer. I was nineteen and at the highest of highs. But at that moment I watched my family implode, and every truth I'd ever known about them was shattered. It...It was a long way to fall."

"I am so sorry, Aaron." Macie didn't know how to even comfort someone who had gone through something like that. She wrapped her arms around his shoulders and squeezed him in a tight hug.

He lifted one shoulder in a shrug. "It's not pleasant to talk about or relive, but it was a long time ago."

"How did you manage to get past that?"

He laughed a humorless laugh. "Well, I started by walking out of the Olympics right then and vowing never to return. Then I decided to move on to drinking. That seemed like the customary response to a problem of that magnitude. So I went to a bar in the Olympic Village with some teammates and had my first drink. Got drunk, even. Then I went back to my room and puked and was absolutely miserable."

He laughed for real this time. "I had spent my life

fueling my body with the healthiest of foods that would make me capable of being an elite athlete, and drinking felt like dumping poison on what I'd worked so hard for. So the night of my first drink was also the night of my last drink."

He shrugged. "So drinking was out. When I got back home, I decided the best course of action would be to get engaged, so I got right on that."

"Wait, what? Were you seriously engaged?"

Aaron nodded.

"Well, that's a...less conventional way of dealing with grief. I guess it's true when they say that everyone deals with it differently."

"You could say that." Aaron's eyes looked up, thoughtful. "I think I was looking for a way to prove that my parents' marriage was just a terrible, horrible fluke. That marriage wasn't really like that. That real love was possible. That a marriage like I had *thought* my parents had was possible."

"And?"

"Well, finding candidates wasn't a problem. It's not hard to get dates when you have a couple of gold medals tucked away in a drawer." He looked down where his hand rested on the seat not far from hers. "It sounds like that kind of situation would be ideal. A real ego booster.

"But in reality, it just means that you have no idea who likes you for who you are, and who likes you for what you just did and the notoriety it brings. Especially because the press felt the need to get involved in all of it. I actually enjoyed the press back when they were covering my swimming times and my meets. I liked them less when all they could focus on was my parents' divorce and who I dated.

"But then I met Sabrina. She seemed perfect, and I was convinced that she liked me for me. I proposed, she said yes, and we started planning a wedding. We were both twenty."

Somehow in the middle of getting to know Aaron better and him meeting her family and that kiss in the kitchen, she'd managed to forget that he was against the one thing that mattered to her the most. "I'm guessing she didn't restore your faith in marriage." What was she thinking, falling for someone like Aaron, when she'd known he never wanted to get married?

Aaron shook his head. "I found out four months into our engagement that she hadn't broken up with her previous boyfriend. They were still very much together."

"No."

"Yep. So drinking had been a failed way to cope, which I hear is pretty true for everyone. And jumping into an engagement was also a failed coping mechanism. After floundering for a bit, I realized that I had three loves: leading, swimming, and kids. So I came up with the brilliant plan of becoming a teacher so I could teach teens how to be stellar people, set goals, work hard to achieve them, and treat others with respect. It hasn't failed me yet."

She put a hand on his shoulder. "Those kids are lucky to have you."

He squeezed her hand that was on his shoulder and met her eyes. "Thank you for showing me Saturday night that families can be different from the one I've experienced. It restored some of my faith in humanity."

She gave him a smile filled with so many conflicting emotions, not the least of which was the dichotomy between the zing that his hand on hers sent through her body and the fact that he'd said her family had restored his faith in *humanity*, not his faith in families. Or in marriage.

He sat up straight and shifted so he was facing her. "Now, if I haven't scared you off too badly with that story, I was planning to stop by your house tonight to ask a favor."

Macie raised an eyebrow.

"I have a class of overachievers— my AP History class. It's a smaller class of just eleven kids. They're involved in everything— taking every Advanced Placement and Honors and Concurrent Enrollment class offered. They are in every extracurricular, after-school offering imaginable—several clubs each, with most of them in club leadership, sports, National Honor Society, volunteering for charity work and other service opportunities, and some of them even manage to squeeze in after-school jobs.

"Anyway, the end of the semester is this Friday, the last day before Christmas break, and as you can imagine, these kids are out of their minds stressed with end-of-semester projects and making sure they maintain their four-point-oh GPAs."

"Several of my students have mentioned how much dog therapy has helped them." He grinned in a way that told Macie that this was his puppy dog pleading face. "Do you think you could bring yours to my class with these kids tomorrow during fourth period?"

Macie smiled. She didn't know how to help with the betrayal he felt from his parents and his ex-fiancée, but this she could do.

AARON

When Macie texted to say that she was almost at the school, Aaron tossed the remains of his lunch in the faculty room garbage can and hurried outside to meet her in the parking lot. It hadn't snowed for a couple of days, so even though the snow was deep on the lawn and in big mounds at the ends of the parking lot, the parking lot and sidewalks were cleared and dry.

"Good afternoon, my mysterious goddess," he said as he opened her door for her.

"Why thank you, my dashing man." She stepped out of the car and placed a hand on his cheek. It was only for a moment, and such a small gesture, but it still sent warmth coursing through him right in the middle of the Colorado cold.

He lifted out the carrier with the three smaller dogs

and grabbed the cat one with his other hand, while Macie led the two bigger dogs on leashes inside the school.

She glanced over at him. "How do you feel about going to my work Christmas party this Friday?"

"Work party? Like with just you and Emily?"

Macie laughed. "No, actually, it's with all of the Main Street Business Alliance members. Dates aren't required, but I thought it might be fun."

"I would love to." They paused outside the windows of the front office, and Lisa looked up, saw that Macie was with him, and gave him a thumbs up.

The hallways were filled with students chatting with friends at the end of lunch, and as they walked, they were met with a chorus of *Awww* and "Look! Puppies!" People swarmed to them, asking if they could pet the dogs.

"I am so sorry," Aaron said. "I didn't even consider this."

"No problem. I don't think it would be possible for Reese and Lola to get too much attention. The littler dogs and Sam, though"—

Aaron looked at the animals in the carriers. The dogs were yipping and jumping and were getting a little overly excited, and Sam was scratching away at the floor of the carrier. "Make way, coming through," he called out in his *Listen to the teacher* voice. And they did. They still lined the halls and bent down to wave at the dogs as they passed, but they left the middle open, so Aaron led Macie up the stairs and to his classroom like they were in a parade.

Once they were in his room and he'd set the carrier down, he stepped up close to Macie. Close enough to kiss her. But instead, he breathed, "Thanks for coming."

She smiled nervously and then glanced at the door. "Should we be doing this with an audience?"

Lola nosed her way right in between the two of them, forcing the space between them to be wide enough to fit a large Goldendoodle. Aaron chuckled. "It seems Lola has an opinion about that too. And she's probably right." He picked up the dog carrier and took it back into his office. He didn't want to let them out until the students entered the room and he could close the door.

Macie crouched down to take the leash off Reese's collar, so Aaron crouched down and did the same with Lola. "So," she said as she laid the leash on the table that held his little classroom Christmas tree, "how are you?"

"Good. The end of the term is Friday, so I've been preparing the students for their tests tomorrow and grading their end-of-semester projects."

Macie nodded and leaned in to take a closer look at the Christmas tree.

"How about you?" he asked. "How are things going with your business?"

"Good. It's been picking up."

How had things become so awkward between them? It

was like the magic of Saturday night had worn off. He had felt so certain about where he stood with her when they had kissed, but he'd second-guessed it a million times since then. He'd replayed their conversation from that night in his head dozens of times and realized that she hadn't said that she felt the same way about him that he did about her. Actually, he wasn't even sure he'd told her how he felt. So maybe the kiss was all just part of trying to convince her family.

He'd already had enough people in his life who had been fake about their relationships. Why had he thought that doing it on purpose was a good idea? He took a stride closer to her. "Listen—"

"Mr. H!" Cory said as he strolled into the room. "I heard you have a surprise for us!"

Morgan squealed and raced past Cory. "It's true!"

The other students filed in close behind Cory and Morgan, dropping their backpacks and binders at their desks, and then gathering around Reese and Lola. Aaron leaned against his desk right next to where Macie leaned against it, close enough that their arms were touching.

"Reese and Lola are in heaven with all this attention," Macie said.

"And look at the smiles on the students' faces." He watched Macie watching the students, and thought she looked like she was in heaven, too. She had opened the perfect business for her.

The bell rang, and the students dutifully stopped petting the dogs and sat in their seats. It made him chuckle, but he should've seen it coming. So he went up in front of the class and explained how class today was going to be hanging out with the dogs.

"I don't understand," Alecia said. "There isn't going to be a lesson?"

"Nope."

"But the end of the semester is three days away," Kyle said. "Shouldn't we be studying?"

Aaron blew out a breath. The easy-going, fun class he'd had just a couple of weeks ago had grown into a ball of stress. "I purposely scheduled the next test for your class well after the break so you'd have one less thing to study for and worry about. Today, this is for you."

Morgan raised her hand. "But"—

Aaron cut her off. "Alright, listen up class; I've got an assignment for you." They all sat up a little straighter. "I need everyone to come up to the board and grab a marker." Once they all stood at the board, a whiteboard marker poised and ready, he said, "I want you to think about what you've got going on today. Okay, now think about yesterday. And now Wednesday, Thursday, and Friday. Keeping those days in mind, on a scale of one to ten, I want you to write down how stressed out you feel."

He watched as nine of eleven students wrote the number ten on the board. Some big, some small, some with a big circle or square around it, and a couple underlined. Allen was the only one who wrote a nine, and Bethany wrote 837.

He walked up to the board and studied the numbers, then turned to the students. "Stress can be good. It can propel you to action. But stress at this high of numbers is not only unhealthy, but it's also unhelpful. Your assignment over the next..." he glanced at the clock, "hour and thirteen minutes is to work to get that number cut in half. I'll have you report back in at the end of class. Now get to work!"

Macie went with him to his back office, got Zeus, Piper, Cookie, and Sam out of their carriers, and released them into the room. Then Macie pulled a couple of small balls out of her bag and tossed them to a couple of students. Piper lay on the floor as Morgan and LeeAnn petted her. Macie crouched down next to them and said, "I brought some Christmas ribbon. Do you guys want to fancy her up?" The two girls' faces lit up, and she passed them a little container.

When she came back to lean against the desk with Aaron, she said, "If things keep picking up, I might be able to rescue another dog from the shelter to add to the Paws and Relax family." Her face had been so excited when she was telling him, but then the smile fell a bit. "If I decide to buy the building. If I don't, I'll have to find homes for most of these dogs."

"You'll be able to buy it," he said. "I believe in you one hundred percent. Before you know it, you'll have that new shelter dog."

As his kids played with the dogs, he swore he could see the stress fleeing from them. He twined his hand in Macie's and brought it to his lips and kissed her knuckles. "Thank you for doing this. It means a lot to me."

"It's a great idea— I'm glad you thought of it. I think I might add it to what we do at Paws and Relax. There might be other teachers who have students in just as much need. And look at how much the dogs are loving it! And look how adorable Piper is looking with those bows."

A few students were tossing a ball to Lola and Zeus, and Cookie was sitting right on Kyle's shoulder, looking like she was wondering if she might want to climb right on top of his head.

"We should talk about that kiss."

"It was a great kiss," Macie said. "I give it a solid ten out of ten."

Aaron laughed. "You know that wasn't what I meant." He searched her face, trying to see if he could find any answers to his unasked questions. All kinds of emotions flitted across her face, but he couldn't figure them out. He needed words. "For you, was it just something to help convince your family?"

Oof! He exhaled as one of the balls hit him in the stomach.

"Sorry, Mr. H!" Cory called out. "My bad!"

He picked up the ball and threw it back to Cory, and then his eyes went back to Macie's. She searched his face, too, and then whispered, "No."

His face split into a grin. "So it meant something more?"

"I've got it!" Bethany called out, and from the corner of his eye, Aaron saw her race across the floor on her hands and knees toward a ball, before he heard a *thud*.

He jerked forward right as Bethany yelped and backed away from a desk, her hands flying to her nose. It started bleeding almost immediately. Aaron grabbed five or six tissues from the box and rushed to her. "Kyle, get on the classroom phone and let the front office know that I'm bringing Bethany down and that she's going to need the nurse."

He made eye contact with Macie and she said, "You go. I've got this."

Once he got Bethany in with the nurse, he called the phone numbers on record for her parents to explain what happened and to see if they could pick up their daughter. They were both in meetings, but he eventually got her older brother who had just come home from college for Christmas. Aaron stood at the door opening and asked the nurse, "What do you think?"

"Could be broken," she said. "She'll want to see a doctor."

Bethany sobbed.

"Your brother is on his way, and he's going to get you to the doctor and take good care of you."

Bethany nodded, then, muffled through the wad of gauze covering her nose, said, "Mr. Hall, I'm feeling like my stress is even higher than eight-thirty-seven right now. Does that mean I'm going to fail this assignment and get a horrible grade in your class?"

He chuckled and shook his head. "You're not going to fail it. I'll tell you what. I'll give you extra credit for being a trooper."

"Thank you," she croaked out, looking like her injury might be worth it if it meant extra credit. He wasn't sure why extra credit mattered so much to someone who already had a 99.4% in his class, but it looked like it did.

As he was trying to make it back to his class before the bell rang, his phone vibrated, so he pulled it out of his pocket and saw a text from Matt.

> Matt: Can you come over the second you get off work?

He quickly typed in a response.

> Aaron: Is everything okay?

> Matt: Just come.

There was so much Aaron wanted to talk to Macie about. So much time he wanted to spend with her. So much more he wanted to find out. And he really *really* wanted to kiss her again.

He was hoping to get a chance to do at least some of that after all his students left. But when he got to the classroom, there was barely enough time to put the room back in order. Before they left, he had the students erase their old stress rating and replace it with the post-hang-out-with-puppies-during-class score, which he was happy to see were all sixes and lower, except for Bethany's 837 that was still on the board.

Distracted by what could be going on with Matt, he helped Macie get the dogs and cat back to her car, she gave him a quick kiss on the cheek, and he said, "I'm sorry I have to run. I'll call you after I leave Matt's."

And now thoughts of Macie and worry about Matt fought for dominance in his mind. He pulled up to the front of Matt's house, the yard filled with Christmas lights and decorations with the lights still on, even though it was mid-afternoon.

He knocked on Matt's door and heard a shouted, "Come in," so he did. The place was feeling strangely empty. Like some of the furniture was missing, or maybe the things on the walls, but he couldn't quite put his finger on what. It just felt as though the essence of the home was gone. Matt was splayed on the couch, looking unshowered and bedraggled.

"Matt, buddy, what's going on?"

Matt sat up and leaned forward with his elbows on his knees. Aaron sat in the chair across from him and waited.

"Ciara and I are separated. She just left with all her stuff right before I texted you."

Of all the things that had run through his mind of what could be wrong, this didn't even make the list at all. Matt and Ciara were the perfect couple. They were rock solid. "How did this happen? I thought you two were happy together. You always seemed...happy."

"We were! But then I lost my job."

"She left you because you lost your job?"

Matt shook his head. "She wasn't upset about that. Well, she *was* upset that I didn't tell her before our game night last week."

"You didn't tell her? Matt!"

"I know, I know. But I knew she'd ask why I got fired, and I didn't want to tell her."

Dread filled Aaron's stomach like a lead weight. "Matt, why did you get fired?"

He ran his hands over his face, and then ran them through his hair, making it stand up in all directions. "I was caught in a compromising situation in the break room with a co-worker. Subordinate, actually— I'm her boss. *Was* her boss."

Aaron fell back in his chair. All he could manage to say was one word. "Why?"

"I don't even know! Because I'm the biggest idiot on the planet? It's never happened before...It was just that once...And we didn't actually..."

"Matt! Regardless of how far you got before you were caught, you cheated on your wife!"

"I know," Matt said and dropped his head into his hands. "What do I do?"

Aaron took a few slow breaths. "I want to be a good friend and give you good advice. I do. But I'm going to need a few minutes to process this before I can." He stood up, let himself out of the house, and started walking around the block.

MACIE

In preparation to eventually start Paws and Relax, Macie had worked at a pet groomer's in college so she'd learn everything she needed to know. She had mostly used the skill to groom her own dogs, but now that she opened it to the public and had started advertising, business was coming in quickly. If this kept up, she might even be able to get a second employee.

As she trimmed the fur of a poodle named Pebbles, she looked around the back room. If she had a second employee, she could probably turn this part into a place to board animals when people went on vacation, just like she'd envisioned when she'd first leased the building.

And if she opened up boarding, along with everything else she was doing, it'd likely bring in more than enough to justify buying the building.

But all that was just dreaming. There was no way to tell if any of those things would be profitable over the long term, so they couldn't be relied on when making her decision. She just needed more facts! More assurances that things would work out. More certainty that buying the building was the right choice. Because if she couldn't be certain, she couldn't tell her landlord that she wanted to put in an offer.

She glanced at her phone like she had every couple of minutes for the past three hours. Logically, she knew that Aaron could be at Matt's for a while. All night, even. But that didn't stop her heart from a little too often hoping she'd get a call from him. Every couple of minutes, apparently. He had started a conversation in his classroom that she desperately wanted to finish. It seemed like maybe he had felt the same way that she did, but she wasn't sure. She wanted to know for sure.

After Pebbles' owner, a war veteran named Jim, stopped by to pick her up, Macie got a phone call. It wasn't Aaron, but it was Joselyn, and that was just what she needed right now.

"Hey, sis! Are you still at work?"

"Yes, why— do you want to go do something?"

Joselyn laughed. "Yes, actually. I am just leaving the shop right now and was hoping to get the last little bit of Christmas shopping done. It sounds like you would love to go with me."

"I very much would. I'm grabbing my stuff right now."

"That's good because I'm already at your door."

Macie poked her head out of her office and saw Joselyn as she reached the front door, baby Aria in her arms. She waved, then hung up the phone and put on her coat. She let Emily know that she was going to be gone for a couple of hours, and if she wasn't back by closing time, Emily should just close up, and she'd be by shortly after to get Reese and Lola.

Light snow was falling as they walked. Just enough to add a little magic to Main Street, the Christmas lights above shining in the darkness. They took Aria to go touch the poinsettia garlands wrapped around all the handrails on the pedestrian bridges, to see the giant wreath on the clock tower, and watched the creek as the lights from above danced in the water that was starting to form ice crystals where the snow met the slow-moving water. Eventually, they even made it to Wishstones and started shopping.

"Okay, tell me what's up," Joselyn said as they paused next to the boxes of wrapping paper. "You've checked your phone dozens of times since we've been out."

She had? And here she thought she had been doing a good job of distracting herself. "I was just hoping for a call from Aaron."

"Here," Joselyn said, putting Aria in her arms. "You

need something to keep your hands busy, and I need to find the perfect paper. You'll hear it when he calls."

Macie made faces at her little niece and was rewarded with some big smiles and a few laughs.

"You really like him, don't you?"

Macie sighed. "I really do. I'm just unsure about how much he likes me."

"Are you kidding? It's obvious how in love with you he is!"

Not really. It was painfully un-obvious.

Joselyn stopped searching through the rolls of wrapping paper and narrowed her eyes, scrutinizing Macie's face. "Why are you so unsure? Did he say or do something? Because from what I saw on Saturday, you two were both looking pretty smitten."

Macie reached down into Joselyn's bag, grabbed a toy, and handed it to Aria. She looked at Aria for a moment as the baby squealed in delight and then started shaking the toy, and then she took a deep breath and looked at her sister. The two of them used to argue a lot back when they were in middle school, but by the time Macie was a sophomore in high school and Joselyn was a senior, they had become best friends. She was used to telling Joselyn everything.

And right now she needed to be real with her sister and to get some help figuring things out way more than she needed to have her believe that she and Aaron were dating.

"I'm unsure because..." She hadn't realized how difficult it would be to tell her sister that she had been lying to her. But if it was so hard, why had it not been so hard to pull off faking the relationship in front of her? Macie wondered if that possibly meant that she hadn't been faking. Maybe she had liked him since that first day. "Okay, remember that day when we first met and were eating ice cream together in your shop?"

Her sister nodded, her hands still frozen on the rolls of wrapping paper.

"I was complaining about dating and said I wanted to take a break for six months. He said he didn't want to ever get married, but his students were set on finding him a wife by the end of the school year. So we decided to fake date each other so that everyone would back off."

"You've been faking?!"

"Shhh!" Macie said. "I don't exactly want it to be public knowledge!"

In a much quieter voice, Joselyn added, "And you didn't tell me?"

"I am so sorry. It was just somehow easier to pull off if I was acting the same way around everyone. I'm not exactly proficient in lying or faking things, so if only the two of us knew, then it was us teaming up together to do something. And he is great to team up with."

"But then you fell for him."

"Pretty fully. I haven't felt this way since..." Macie racked her brain, trying to figure out when, "probably Jack."

Joselyn smiled, remembering. "Wow. When was that? The summer after your senior year? I remember, he was the guy you thought you'd ride off into the sunset with. This is huge."

"Well, huge for me. I have no idea where he stands. But that kiss Saturday night felt pretty real."

"From what Janet, Sophie, Trevor, and Mindy said, it was pretty smoochie-smoochie."

Macie blushed, still embarrassed that her nieces and nephew had witnessed it. "And then earlier today, he started to ask me about it, and it seemed that maybe he had felt something too, but then his students needed him, and then his friend needed him, and I just don't know." She adjusted the way Aria was sitting on her hip and pulled out her phone, just to make sure she hadn't missed the ringtone or the buzz.

Joselyn pulled out two different wrapping paper rolls and held them next to each other, her head cocking to the side. "Well, from where I stood, things looked pretty authentic on his part. Do you think you want to continue dating him— for real?" Joselyn must've decided on the paper because she moved down the aisle to the bows.

"I don't know. I like him a lot. For so many reasons.

But I've found myself hoping again, and that's a dangerous thing. It's like my heart has PTSD when it comes to hope. It knows that when it starts to hope, it has to prepare for being shattered."

"Unless this is the one time that it doesn't get shattered. Maybe this will be what restores your heart's faith in hope." She picked up a box of bows, and then looked toward the front of the store. "We really should've grabbed a cart if we want to get any shopping done."

They headed to the front of the store, then Macie buckled Aria into the seat in the cart and handed back the toy she had tossed onto the ground. "I think shattering is the more likely outcome. Plus, I think I've been getting signs all along that we shouldn't be together."

Joselyn crossed her arms and raised an eyebrow in only the way an older sister could.

"No, really. Every time we've been together, something bad has happened. That first day, we went to the tree lighting, remember? And for the first time in probably all of Nestled Hollow history, the tree lighting caused a power outage for the entire city."

"That's because it was the first time in Nestled Hollow history that we had that many lights on the tree."

"At Winter Formal, we got the kids dancing, and one danced into the refreshment table, and punch and cookies went everywhere. At the hayride, that little kid got separated from his mom, so I got us disqualified." She tried to think through the order of the dates they'd gone on. "And then at his friend's house, not only did we have to leave early because I was getting so sick, but I totally and completely offended and embarrassed his friend. At the family Christmas party, we all got snowed in."

"Which ended up working in your favor, if you remember. Plus, the kids had a blast with the bonus sleepover."

"Today," she plowed ahead, sure that if she presented enough evidence, Joselyn would understand, "I took the dogs to his AP History class, and one of the girls got a broken nose. A broken nose, from playing with my dogs! What are the chances of that even happening?"

Joselyn still had her arms crossed and they still hadn't moved from the front of the store. Macie grabbed hold of the handle of the shopping cart and steered it back toward the toy section of the store, so Joselyn followed. "Oh! And let's not forget the first moment we met— it was because Lola ran ahead and her leash caused him to crash his bike. We met because he *crashed*."

"Maybe the crash happened because neither of you would've given each other a chance if it hadn't."

Macie just shook her head. "There has just been too much evidence that it's a bad idea. I mean seriously, Joselyn, even the idea was bad, because when I went to Best Dressed, I wasn't even with Aaron. I was simply getting a dress for when I would be with him, and chaos erupted at Paws and Relax just during those few minutes I was gone."

Joselyn reached out and stopped the cart, stopping Macie. "Or maybe you're just looking for reasons."

Macie sighed. "The fact remains that my goal is to get married. His goal is to not get married. So none of this matters anyway. My brain should've known all along not to let hope in because there's no hope to be had when it comes to things working out between us. Subconsciously, my brain hasn't been doing its job of protecting my heart from harm. I need to start doing it consciously."

Joselyn shook her head like she saw that Macie was just going down a path she'd seen her go down before. But this one was different. "Just...Before you decide to do that, wait for his call. Ask him your questions, and see what he has to say, okay? Just wait for that?"

Macie hesitated, so Joselyn said, "Your 'boyfriend' and you have been fake dating, and you *didn't tell me*. I think the least you could do to make up for that is to promise me you'll wait until he calls to decide anything."

Macie nodded. She could do that. "Okay, I will."

Except Aaron didn't call at all that night.

Or at all on Wednesday or Thursday.

By the time Friday morning rolled around and her texts were still going unanswered, she wasn't even sure they were going to be going to the Main Street Business Alliance Christmas party together.

sixteen

AARON

Aaron knew he should've called Macie or responded to her texts. But Matt's news had hit him hard, and he'd barely managed to stay focused enough to make it through the last few days of school. If he'd been dating any girl other than Macie, he'd have already texted, letting them know that he was out— that he couldn't date right now.

But this was Macie.

So Friday during lunch, when he only had one class period left before the semester was over and school let out for two weeks for the Christmas break, he finally felt strong enough to reply. Before today, he'd planned to let her know that he couldn't make it to her work Christmas party, but now that the day was here, he decided that maybe he could handle it. Plus, he just really wanted to see her. He typed out a text and pressed send.

> Aaron: I apologize for not calling. It's been a rough few days. Are we still on for tonight?

The text showed as being read, but it was still a few agonizing minutes before the bubble showing that she was replying appeared.

> Macie: I'm sorry about your last few days! If you need to skip tonight, that's okay. As I said, dates aren't required, and I don't mind going alone.

> Aaron: I want to go. What time and where should I meet you?

> Macie: 8:00, at the library on Main Street. Go around to the back, and you'll see doors that lead to the basement.

He knew he should've offered to pick her up so that they could arrive together, but he just didn't have it in him.

———

Aaron arrived at the doors to the basement of the library just a few minutes after eight, took a deep breath, and went inside. Macie's face lit up when she saw him, but then fell pretty soon after. This was a party. He needed to figure out how to smile while he was here. He worked on it while she made her way to him.

"How are you doing?"

"I've been better. Matt told me that he cheated on Ciara, so of course Ciara moved out a couple of days ago."

Macie gasped. "Oh no. But they seemed so happy!"

He didn't know why he brought it up. He didn't want to talk about it— he mostly just wanted her to understand why he wasn't feeling the Christmas spirit. He shifted his gaze to the Christmas tree and a refreshments table instead of at Macie. She picked up that he didn't want to talk about it pretty quickly.

"Come," she said. "You need punch." She led him to the table, seeming a little unsure of herself, but covering it decently well. As she was ladling the punch into a cup, she said, "I know you don't want alcohol to harm this beautiful body of yours so I'd reassure you by letting you know this punch doesn't contain any, but it probably does have a near-lethal amount of sugar, so there's that."

She smiled so big when she was handing it to him that he couldn't help but smile while he took it, his hand lingering on the cup, brushing up against hers longer than necessary.

"I think I could use the sugar today."

Macie led him around the room, introducing him to

everyone. In his current state, it made him seriously question whether he should've come.

The woman with auburn hair who had been taking pictures at Hayride of the Santas stood in front of an area where chairs were set up, wearing a shirt that said, *I'm dreaming of a white (and black and read) Christmas*, and had a picture of a rolled up newspaper under a Christmas tree. She called out, "Everyone come on over— it's time for our first game!"

Macie leaned in and whispered, "Are you sure you want to stay?"

He nodded, grabbed her hand, and headed to the chairs. He had needed something to get his mind off Matt, and maybe this would do it.

"For this first game, everyone's going to need a partner, so if you didn't bring someone, find someone to be yours."

Macie looked at him and batted her eyes. Bad mood or not, she still managed to get a laugh out of him. "Will you do me the honor of being my partner in this game?"

"That would make me as happy as a kid who just found out he made the 'nice' list."

Aaron's eyes went back to the front, where the woman said, "This game is called 'TV Art Show Host,' and you guys are the artist hosting! The always incredible Eli, here, is going to help me demonstrate."

A man came up and joined her, and by the way they

looked at each other, they were dating. Or married. He glanced down at their ring fingers. Ahh. Engaged.

"Okay, the taller person goes in the front— that's you, honey— and the shorter one behind." They scooted closer to a giant notebook of paper, the kind teachers sometimes used, that was propped up on an easel. "The taller person is the voice, and the shorter person is the arms, and cannot talk. The taller person puts their hands behind their backs, and the shorter person puts their arms under the arms of the person in front and sticks them out like this." Eli was facing the audience, but the woman's arms were the only arms they saw, and she waved at the crowd, making it look like Eli was the one waving.

"When it's your partnership's turn up here, I'll show the shorter person a paper that says what scene they are going to draw, and what things need to be in it. Since they're shorter, they aren't going to be able to see what they're drawing. While they're drawing, the taller person has to narrate what's happening, as if they are the host of a show that is teaching the audience how to draw this scene. And since the taller person can't see what's on the paper, they're just going to have to figure it out as they go. Now, who wants to be first?"

Everyone looked around at each other like they weren't sure if they wanted to start a game they'd never played before, including Macie and Aaron.

"Okay then, I nominate..." The woman looked around the crowd. "Macie!"

"Thanks, Whitney," Macie said, then looked at Aaron. "What do you say, teammate? We've partnered up on everything else pretty well."

"True. Let's win this. Is this a game where there are winners?"

"Even if it isn't, let's win it anyway."

They went to the front of the crowd, and Eli adjusted the giant notepad so that everyone could see it. Aaron put his hands behind his back, and Macie slid her arms between his arms and his sides, and the touch sent heat rushing to his chest. Whitney showed Macie a paper, and he felt Macie lean back just enough to read it, then she closed the gap between them.

"Welcome," Aaron said, turning to face the group, "to today's episode of Draw a Christmas Scene. I am your host and resident artist..." He tried to quickly think of a couple's name for him and Macie while she spread her arms out like he was about to introduce something awesome. "Aaracie." Okay, that one was awful. Maybe he should've thought about this first. He turned his back most of the way toward the group so that he was facing the big sheet of paper.

"I'd like to tell you what scene we're drawing today, but I thought it might be more fun to keep it a surprise. Oh, and we're drawing. For those of you following along at home, we are starting by drawing two horizontal lines right in the middle of the paper. And then some vertical lines— one on the left side and one, um, kind of in the center? Never mind. Scribble that one out. We don't make mistakes here; we make happy little scribbles, like a garland on a Christmas tree. Doesn't that just add to the festiveness?"

After spending a full four days away from Macie, away from her family, and in the middle of the mess made by someone he trusted more than anyone in the world, he'd been ready to walk away. But seeing her here today brought everything back.

"Next, kind viewers and budding artists, we draw a box underneath the horizontal lines. Oh, and then inside the box, but also kind of outside the box, we are drawing... Actually, I'm not going to tell you just yet, I'm going to let you have a moment to see if you can guess. If you're doing this at home, just make things that kind of look like rectangles, but with the short sides curved, and just throw a bunch in there at all different angles. Now draw a jagged line above, kind of like the teeth of a shark. Oh! And that, my friends, is how you draw logs and a fire in a...I'm pretty sure that's a fireplace."

And feeling her pressed up against his back like this made him want to turn around and hold her tight and never let go. He wanted to lean into her, to have that cheek she had laying on his back to be laying on his chest. He wanted to kiss the top of her head.

"Okay, now above the fireplace, I want you to draw a big circle. That's right, don't worry if where you started the circle doesn't match up with where you ended. It's those kinds of details that give this artwork personality. Now inside the circle, in the... bottom half, it looks like, draw a circle that's less than half the size of the bigger one. Then above it, draw two smaller circles. Now see how great that looks, having a giant face above your fireplace, giving you the *Wow* look?"

Everything to do with Macie right now confused him. Things were no longer clean and clear in his mind— it was all one muddled mess. He couldn't figure out if he desperately wanted to be with her, or if he desperately wanted to run away. All he knew was he loved being with her. And that being with her was scaring him senseless. And the one person he would usually go to when he needed to talk things through, Matt, was the very last person he could go to.

"Wait a moment, we're adding more eyes to the face. And more eyes." He could feel Macie laughing into his back. "Lots more eyes. Yep, a *Wow* face with lots of eyes. That's the secret to drawing a wreath hanging above your fireplace!"

He knew what Macie wanted. All along he'd known what he wanted. But then getting to know Macie and being around her family had made him question that. It made him want what he hadn't wanted since he'd first separated from Sabrina. It made him want a wife who would be with him through thick and thin, facing all of life side by side. It made him feel like he might have been wrong about marriage all these years.

"But don't stop yet young artists," he said, "because we have a few more details to add. Yes, right in the middle of your canvas, we want to add a squirrely line. Remember what I said about that adding festiveness? Oh, wait. We don't want to stop at the squirrely line; we want to curve it around and I think we maybe wanted to keep going until we get sort of in the vicinity of the beginning of the line. Because then when we're done, we'll have... a lump of coal, maybe? Those things are flammable, so don't keep your lumps of coal this close to the fire in your own homes, young artists."

Seeing what happened with Matt's and Ciara's marriage made him realize he hadn't been wrong, though. He should've known better than to turn his back against guards he'd had in place for a reason. Guards he'd had for years. They were there to protect him, and he had let himself tear them down. He could already feel the pain that was causing and knew from experience how much more it could inflict.

"Keep going with those and pretty soon, you'll have three very lovely...stockings! Yes, three lovely stockings hanging on or floating above— your choice— your mantle. He turned to face the group and said, "And now we've reached the end of our episode. I do hope you'll join us next time when we discover how to draw a new and very unique Christmas scene. Until then," he could no longer remember the couple name he'd used for them, so he paused, trying to figure something out, "this is Macron, signing out."

Macie spread her arms wide and he took a bow. The group roared with laughter and cheered. Macie came out from behind him and they grasped hands and did a second bow. She grinned at him, and he grinned right back and wished that partnering with Macie— in every random way they had over the past few weeks— didn't always come so naturally. Because having so much fun with her just muddied the waters even more than they already were. Why couldn't she just be awful? That would make this so much easier.

seventeen

MACIE

After three and a half days of not hearing from Aaron and her heart aching to connect with him, she was happy that he had texted that they were still on for the Main Street Business Alliance party. She was also more than a little wary. She had been hoping that he liked her more than just as a fake date, but three and a half days of no texting was a pretty big sign that he probably didn't.

Of course, she figured that those days of no contact could very well have been because of what was going on with his friend Matt, but thinking along those lines was the same as holding out hope. And she was working to keep herself far from hope.

Still, though, she had hoped for some kind of answers. But all night long, she had been getting the opposite of answers. When Aaron had first arrived, he'd seemed like he didn't want to be there at all. He was gracious enough as she was introducing him to everyone, but his usual spark was gone. Was that spark something he normally had, even when he wasn't around her, and other things had taken it away? Or was that a spark that was a special reserved-for-her spark, and whatever connection they'd had was now gone?

She didn't know him outside of having close contact with him, so she had no idea what his usual was. All she knew was that her fears and doubts aside, she missed the old Aaron.

And then, during the Art Show Host game, he returned. He was back, *and* she had gotten to snuggle up to him. The smells of cinnamon and pine and chlorine and something else that was so uniquely and so perfectly Aaron that had clung to his coat was right next to her, and she had basked in it. Having him near her was so much better than having his coat. And he'd been fun and they'd worked together so well, just like they always had, and she'd felt connected to him again. She'd even put a second check mark next to *Will do crazy, spontaneous things with me*.

But after they sat back down, that disappeared. A few more pairs went up to do the Art Show Host game, and they'd all laughed pretty heartily, but his spark was gone again. Confused and frustrated by the mixed signals of apathy and fun and disappointment and irritability that were coming off him in constantly changing but buffeting waves, she got up and went to the refreshment table. Maybe some liquid sugar would help.

Actually, what she needed was water. Cool, clean water. And a walk in the brisk outdoor air. She tried to think of something in her car that she could say she forgot and had to run outside to get it. Maybe the cold air would help her think.

Before she came up with something, though, Aaron was at her side. She had so many questions for him and suddenly couldn't think of a single one. But then he stood there, sparkless and unreadable, and she knew exactly what she needed to ask. "Do you like me?"

So many conflicting emotions played on his face so quickly that she couldn't tell which one was strongest. After a moment, he carefully said, "Yes."

"Fake-like me or real-like me?"

"Real." Again with the careful, one-word answers.

One-word answers she *didn't* want to hear. What she wanted to hear him say was that he didn't actually like her —it was all a show, just like they had planned. Because if that was the case, then she could easily abandon all hope in this relationship because that's what she'd been after all along. An escape from hoping something would work out.

But he just gave her a yes. Knowing that, was this relationship one she could move forward with? She didn't know if it was even possible. There were too many obstacles standing in their way. Not the least of which was the fact that he looked like he was pretty unhappy about liking her. Almost like he was mad about it.

He opened his mouth like maybe he wanted to ask a question. The same one she had asked him, possibly? But then he closed it, grabbed a cup of punch, and kept his eyes on it.

Macie said, "Your words are telling me one thing, but your actions"—

At the same time, Aaron said, "I don't know if I can"—

But just as both of them stopped talking to let the other talk, Brooke stepped up to the refreshment table. "Hello, you two! How are you...Oh."

Just then, the whole group started making their way over. Macie was not about to advertise the troubles she and Aaron were having to all of her peers, and she didn't want to put Aaron on the spot when he was struggling enough just talking to her about what was bothering him. So she pasted on a smile, even though it felt forced and not resembling a smile. "Is the game finished?" She slid her hand into Aaron's as a wordless plea for help, because she knew she wasn't pulling this off well on her own at all.

In a swift movement, he pulled his hand out of hers. "I'm sorry. If you'll all excuse me, I need to leave. Right now."

He hurried to the chairs at the side of the room where all the coats were stacked and pulled his out of the pile.

"Oh," Cole said. "We're sad to see you leave early. It's been fun having you."

It took a moment before Macie recovered from the shock of Aaron's sudden reaction. Then she rushed to the chairs and pulled out her coat, and ran after Aaron as he opened the door and went out into the cold night.

"Aaron!" she called out.

He stopped in his tracks and then turned to face her. "I'm sorry. I really am."

"What just happened in there?"

Aaron ran his hands over his face. "I wasn't lying when I said I liked you. More than like, actually. And I thought that maybe we could make it work, but then I realized that the chances of it working were pretty minuscule."

He took a few deep breaths before continuing. "Seeing my parents broadcast a fake relationship to the world when in reality it was decayed, and then going through it again with Sabrina took me somewhere more agonizing than I had known existed. And then the thing happened with Matt. I had forgotten how painful it is." He swallowed. "He reminded me why I never wanted to get married."

Macie tried to figure out how she should respond to that, but words didn't come. She just stood there, mouth slightly open, but silent.

"And then seeing you in there, pretending everything

between us was fine when it very clearly wasn't— it was just too much. I couldn't."

"I wasn't trying to"—

He stepped closer, putting up a hand. "No, I know. But I can't" — He paused, searching her face. "I just...I'm sorry. I can't." Then he turned and walked away.

AARON

The saying "misery loves company" must be true because there wasn't another good explanation of why Aaron ended up on Matt's doorstep at eleven A.M. on Saturday with a pizza in one hand and chicken wings in the other.

"She's just so perfect," Matt said. "How could I have forgotten for a second how perfect she was? Do you think there's ever going to be another woman as perfect as Ciara? I'll tell you right now there's not."

"Just like there's never going to be another woman I get along with as well as Macie."

"You two were pretty fun together. You pair up well."

"We really did. I've never had that before. In all the girls I've dated, and you know that's been a lot—"

"By-product of never getting serious."

"—none of them has been a *teammate* before. Someone who felt like a partner, who stood side-by-side with me in whatever we happened to be facing."

"That's valuable stuff, man."

"It really is."

"And we threw it all away."

"Because we're stupid."

A knock sounded at the door, and Matt called out, "Whatever you're selling, we're not interested!"

There was another knock, more persistent this time. Aaron would've gotten up to get it, but he'd been half sitting, half laying in this same uncomfortable position for a while, and it'd take more effort than he could muster to move. A moment later, the door opened, and Ian & Timini, Dennis & Julie, and Shad & Annah all walked in.

"Ew," Timini said. "How long has this pizza been sitting here?"

Matt glanced up at the clock on the wall. "Like six hours. What are you guys doing?"

"Getting you lowlifes off the couch," Shad said as he opened the curtains. Aaron and Matt both shielded their eyes from the brightness of the setting sun.

Ian kicked the bottom of Aaron's shoe, making his leg move from where it had been resting for way too long. "I expect Matt to wallow. No offense, Matt."

Matt raised a hand. "None taken."

"But not you, Aaron. This isn't like you at all."

He shrugged. It wasn't like him. "Well, I've never thrown away a chance at a real relationship with someone like Macie before, so it seemed appropriate."

"Up," Julie said, offering her hand to help pull him up. "We all know you don't go Christmas shopping until school gets out for the break, so we're going to take you."

Dennis held a hand out to Matt. "Because we know if we don't, none of us will be getting presents from you turkeys."

———

It felt good to get out around people in the one department store in Mountain Springs. And to move his legs again, see bright lights, and talk to people who weren't as miserable as he and Matt were.

All though it felt *good*, it still didn't feel *right*. Macie had redefined what "right" was for him, without him even realizing that it happened. He was twenty when his engagement to Sabrina ended. Here he was, a full nine years later, and he was pretty sure that he was worse at dealing with a breakup now. Should he be missing Macie this much? He had only known her for a few weeks, after all. But the impact she'd left on him was so much greater.

He'd only brought her to his city once. Yet everything here reminded him of her. A dress on display in the center aisle was almost the same color of blue as the one Macie had worn at Winter Formal when they'd danced like they'd been dancing together their whole lives. In a Lego display, he saw the same set they'd gotten the little boy during Hayride of the Santas. The shoe section reminded him of running barefoot in Dennis and Julie's backyard. Some Christmas stockings hanging on a printed cardboard cutout reminded him of the picture they'd drawn at her work party. And of the stockings hanging on her parents' mantle.

Maybe he would never get over her.

"So, I was talking with Ciara," Annah said, and Matt straightened like he was on full alert. "She said she might be open to going to marriage counseling with you."

"What?" He grabbed Annah's shoulders. "She really said that?"

Annah smiled. "I'm sure it will take some heavy-duty repentance on your part."

"And major, major groveling," Ian added.

"And never even *thinking* about another woman again," Timini said.

"You hurt her a lot," Annah said. "And that's not going to be an easy or quick thing to get over. But deep down, she still loves you. And before all this happened, you two had something special."

"Do everything you can to make things right," Ian said. "Keep doing them until you can convince yourself and her that there's no chance it'll happen again, and you never know. You might get a second chance."

Matt practically floated down the aisle, but Aaron stayed at the back of the group, lagging behind everyone else. Julie slowed to Aaron's speed and bumped her shoulder into his. "You're being awfully quiet."

"I'm just surprised, I guess. Why would Ciara even think of taking him back?"

She shrugged. "Sometimes things aren't as broken and unfixable as they can appear to be."

nineteen

MACIE

Paws and Relax still needed Macie. The animals still needed Macie. Emily still needed Macie. So she went to work on Saturday like she always did. She gave all the shoppers chances to relax and recover and prepare for their second trip into the fray. She gave little kids who were stir-crazy from being strapped into shopping carts too long a chance to run and play with pets. And she gave people who were saddened by the holidays a chance to brighten their day.

And then she took Reese and Lola home, walked straight to her room, and shut the door behind her.

She wasn't sure how much later— a couple of hours, maybe?— Marcus knocked on her door. "We're about to watch a movie. Come join us."

She didn't respond.

"It'll do you good." He paused. "Come on, Macie. Emily said you shut yourself in your office at work whenever you could, too."

Macie grabbed a blanket out of her closet, walked out of her room, put her coat, gloves, scarf, hat, and boots on, and then walked out the back door. She walked out to where the snow was nice and deep and untouched, spread the blanket out right on top of the snow, and then flopped down on it, the snow beneath her forming to her body, feeling as close to lying on a cloud as she could imagine.

There. She was out of her room.

Her breaths made little cloud puffs in front of her face as she stared up at the stars, Christmas music wafting across the backyards of her family. It was probably coming from Everett's house. She heard songs a little further away, coming from Christmas carolers at one of her neighbors'.

A few minutes later, light spilled onto the snow from the back door. She closed her eyes, hoping it wasn't Marcus or Joselyn coming out to talk. A moment later, though, Reese leaped onto the blanket with her, wearing his booties so his paws wouldn't get too cold in the snow. She sat up to say thank you, but she only saw the back door close.

Reese seemed to know exactly what she needed— someone to just be next to her as she grieved, and to have zero expectations. He stretched his body out next to hers, and she petted the fur at his neck.

"I really liked him, Reese." She took a few slow breaths. "And because I know you won't tell anyone, I'll confide in you that I think maybe I even loved him. Okay, I know I loved him, and I loved him a lot. I think I started falling in love on that very first day, but I wasn't willing to admit it, because it wasn't part of the plan.

"And now he's gone."

Reese whined, and Macie wrapped her arms around his neck and hugged him tightly.

"He was just unlike anyone I've ever dated. I mean, it's not like I've never dated anyone where we connected in the way we have fun before. Or connected in the way we work in a partnership. Or connected in the way we treat kids. It's just I've never experienced all of that with the same person before. Plus, you saw us, Reese. Standing next to each other, we just look like we belong together, don't you think?"

Reese barked and then licked her neck. Macie chuckled and rubbed behind his ears.

"Remember how I said that I wasn't going to hope? Zero hope for six months. I said that, right? Well, I guess I opened the door just a teeny crack, and when I wasn't looking, hope snuck its way in. And I'm talking about a *lot* of it. I didn't even realize how much had gotten in until Aaron broke things off yesterday."

She turned her face toward the stars again and listened as the Christmas carolers started a new song, to the east of where they were before.

"What do I do, Reese? What do you do when you've been searching for your needle in a haystack ever since high school, so for nine years, and then right when you give up, you feel one in your hand, and you think it might be your actual needle? And before you've even had enough of a chance to bask in the sunlight that's glinting off the needle, it disappears, *poof!* right out of your hand." Reese whimpered and nuzzled in a little closer.

She looked off to the side, twisting to see the empty lot that was hers, covered in a blanket of untouched snow.

"What do you say, Reese? You and I can build a house there. We'll find you a wife— an adorable, stalwart lab who will stand by your side, and the two of you can have a houseful of puppies. We'll find a great husband for Lola, too, and they can have a bunch of puppies, and all your puppies can romp and wrestle and play together like they're cousins. And then every time I'm sad that I don't have my own spouse and houseful of kids, you can just come to lay next to me and listen to me and whine at all the right places because you're super good at that."

Reese rolled onto his stomach and put a paw on her shoulder, and just looked at her like he understood. Then he leaned his head forward and licked her cheek, wiping off a tear that had slipped out, making her laugh. "Okay, you know you just left my cheek wetter than it was, right? You're a good boy, Reese. Thanks for always being by my side."

twenty

AARON

Aaron finished his Christmas shopping during the day of Christmas Eve. Alone. That had never bothered him before— he enjoyed doing things in groups, but he had always been perfectly fine doing pretty much anything solo. But today somehow felt like a window into his future. A future where his friends were with their spouses, off to visit family, and he was alone.

Braving the traffic and the crowds of last-minute shoppers, he headed to the closest mall on the outskirts of Denver. He had just bought the last gift on his list when he felt his phone buzzing. He pulled it out of his pocket and looked at his screen. It was his sister Aliza.

He frowned at the screen. He, his sister, his mom, and his dad always did a group video call on Christmas day. That way, they all didn't have to make multiple calls to get in their obligatory chat with everyone, and if there was a lag in the conversation, there were four people to fill it instead of just two. His sister didn't just call out of the blue like this. He hoped that everything was okay.

"Hello?"

"Hey, big brother."

"Hi, Aliza. Is everything okay?"

"Can't a girl call her big brother on Christmas Eve even if nothing is wrong?"

"She can call anytime. It's just a little unprecedented."

"Well, you know me— I like being unpredictable. How deep is the snow in icicle-land?"

"A few inches above my knees. How hot's the oven in Phoenix?"

"A little chilly, actually. Sixty-eight. Although if you were here, I bet you'd be wearing shorts, even though it looks like it might rain."

Aaron laughed. "Probably."

"Okay, enough with the idle chit-chat. I called for a real reason, and I wanted to tell you before the family video chat."

Aaron paused a moment, then realized he was stopping right in the middle of the hallway of the mall and kept walking. "I'm listening."

"A while ago, I met a guy. His name is Frederick, and he's pretty great. We've been dating for most of this year, and Saturday night he proposed to me right below the lanterns at Lights of the World."

"You're...*engaged?*" Aaron spotted a chair five feet away and practically fell into it.

"Can you believe it? One of the offspring of Ken and Sheri Hall somehow survived their parents' fiasco of a divorce and is going to get married."

"An impressive feat indeed. I'd like to offer my congratulations. You sound really happy."

"I am. Thank you."

"Aren't you worried that—what?" Aaron's attention flew to the man standing in front of him with his hands on his hips, wearing an elf suit.

"You're in my seat," the angry elf said.

Aaron looked around and noticed for the first time that he'd fallen into a seat in Santa's court, where kids were lined up to sit on Santa's lap, surrounded by giant-sized candy canes and lollipops and gumdrops. And the seat he was sitting in looked more like a throne than the mall benches nearby.

"Oh, sorry. Here you go. Merry Christmas."

He grabbed his bags and started walking again.

"Aaron? What's going on?"

"Nothing. Except I think an elf just put my name on the naughty list. Okay, so you're engaged. Don't you worry that things might turn out like they did for Mom and Dad?"

"Or like they did for you and Sabrina?"

"I like that you don't tiptoe around subjects that might be sensitive."

"You know me, bro. I call it as I see it. Besides, it's been nine years. I figured you were over it by now."

"I am. It's just that all that kind of stuff resurfaced lately, so it feels fresh."

"Uh oh. Do you want to talk about it?"

"This call is about you, not me." He pushed open the outside doors and headed into the parking lot.

"Okay, you asked if I worry that my marriage will turn out like Mom's and Dad's, and the answer is no. It's a worry I've had pretty much constantly in the past, though. I'm a drop-dead gorgeous dancer with an MBA— this wasn't the first time I've been proposed to. A couple of them were great guys, too. Ones who would've made pretty fantastic husbands.

"But this is the first time where I felt like not only was he a great guy, but a great guy for me specifically. And it was the first time where I felt like I had gotten past the way I got screwed up as a teenager going through Mom's and Dad's divorce."

"So there's a way to get past that then?" He pushed the button on his key fob to pop his trunk and then put his bags inside.

"There is. It kind of surprised me, too. I mean, there's not a magic way or anything. A lot of it just happened over time. It probably has for you, too, and you just haven't realized it. I just got to a point where I realized that I am not Mom and Dad. Frederick is not Mom and Dad. They faced some challenges, sure. But they chose to put other things before each other, and I've chosen not to. I'm marrying someone who is just as dedicated as I am to putting each other first. When we're faced with challenges, we aren't going to make the same mistake."

Aaron opened his car door and got inside. "And he's a good guy?"

"One of the best I've ever known. This woman who's on your mind"—

"I never said there was a woman."

"Well, maybe not with your actual words, but it's coming across loud and clear. Is she a good person?"

He put the key in the ignition but didn't turn it. "The very best there is."

"A decade ago, Mom and Dad caused us a lot of pain, and I think we've both been carrying it around with us. It's kind of scary to lay down a load that's become a part of who we are. But Aaron?"

"Yeah?"

"It also feels pretty great. People aren't meant to be alone. It took me a long time to realize that applies to me, too."

Aaron had always figured it didn't apply to him, either. And before Macie, he was perfectly fine with being alone.

She had opened a door in him that hadn't ever been opened before, and now he wasn't sure if he'd ever be fine being alone again. Could he lay down that pain he'd been carrying with him? It had become a big part of who he was. Did he dare lay it down and walk away from it? Could he have enough faith and trust in himself and in Macie to believe that they could make it work?

"Thank you, Aliza. Out of all the people who could've helped me figure things out, I would've never guessed the best advice would come from family."

"Remember when you were going through your big breakup and we used to talk all the time?"

"Yeah."

"We should do that again. If I've learned anything in the past few weeks, it's that family matters. I would love to have a more than twice-a-year brother."

Family mattered. It's something he had just begun to learn, too. "I would like that too." He thought about what Macie's dad had said when they put up the stockings at their Christmas Kickoff party. *Your relationships with your family matter.* He'd told them the importance of talking things out and fixing things and nurturing each other. That relationships take work, but it was the most valuable work he could do. That it was important to keep those links strong.

Aaron now knew that it was important with his own

family, and it was important with the woman he wanted to become family.

He turned the key in the ignition and let the phone call switch over to the car. "Thank you, Aliza. I'm really glad you called. Now if you'll excuse me, I've got to go—I've got to get in touch with someone. I might call you before the family video chat tomorrow."

Aliza paused, and then said, "Before?" with a little too much excitement and question behind the word.

"Maybe. I guess it all depends on how good I am at apologizing and making up for being a complete jerk to someone who didn't deserve it, and in convincing her of how much I love her."

"Then I'll be rooting for before."

twenty-one

MACIE

Macie walked into her room, carrying bags filled with all the papers from her office. She pulled her phone out of her pocket when it buzzed, looked at the text, and groaned before tossing all the bags on her bed.

"Not a happy text?" Joselyn asked from the doorway.

"It's Max Cohen. He said that he's not trying to rush me, but he'd like to start preparing everything for the building to go up for sale on January first if I'm not going to put in an offer, so the sooner I let him know the direction I'm going, the better. He's hoping for a quick sale."

"And have you decided what you're going to do?"

"I just don't see how I can put in an offer. But if I tell him no, what do I do with the animals when the building sells? I've looked, and haven't found a location to move the business to. Do I just close up shop and have the animals I rescued from the shelter go back there?" The whole thing made her stomach churn just thinking about it.

She opened the flap of the bag containing the binders with all her financial information. One more look at the information, and she was going to have to decide. It was Christmas Eve, which meant she only had one week left, and nothing that happened with the business was going to change drastically during that time to warrant putting the decision off any longer.

Joselyn walked into the room and sat on her bed. "So tell me what you're thinking. And stop giving me that look, because it's been years since I have pulled the older sister card and told you what to do."

"True."

"And not only am I family, but I'm also your *best friend*. And best friends and family talk this kind of stuff out with each other."

Macie sat down cross-legged on the bed facing Joselyn and opened the binder. "Okay. Here's what my monthly income looked like from each of the different programs I run before I started making changes, and here's the one from after."

Joselyn took both of them in her hands, looking back

and forth between the two. "Wow. This is pretty incredible."

Macie nodded. "Part of me is actually kind of grateful that Max gave me a deadline like that because it pushed me to try some things that I had been a little wary of trying. If I would have known they'd work out so well, I would've tried them a while ago. I just wish the deadline didn't also come with me losing my business."

"You're not going to lose your business."

"I don't see how I can keep it. I have no guarantee that these numbers will stay the same month after month. And I have no idea if something will happen with me or the business that I haven't predicted."

Joselyn set the papers aside. "I know you're a good saver. How are your bank accounts looking?"

"For my business account, I have about six months of expenses saved up."

"That's fantastic, Macie. How about your personal accounts?"

Macie handed her the spreadsheet with her personal finance information, and Joselyn's eyes grew big. "Whoa! You've managed to save up that much money? Macie, you could practically pay for two-thirds of the entire building cost with this!"

Panic coursed through Macie at the thought of there not being a big chunk of money sitting in her account, ready for any emergency that came along. She wiped her sweaty palms on her pants and tried to slow her breathing.

"Relax, Macie. I'm not suggesting you should dump it all into your building. I'm just saying that if something happened, you'd have options. This opens so many possibilities."

Macie shook her head. "It's not enough of a safety net. It won't cover everything. There are no guarantees that if I buy the building that bad things won't happen." She looked down at the papers. Papers that she'd been studying for the past three weeks. There were just so many unknowns that she couldn't prepare for.

And the unknowns that she did know to prepare for, like what would happen if she got sick or injured or any of a million things that could stop her from being able to work for more than a day or two, were all things she hadn't made a great plan for yet.

"I think you're letting fear of unclear outcomes stop you from some pretty great things. In both your business and your relationship with Aaron."

Macie's head jerked up. "With Aaron?"

"Oh, come on. Don't tell me you don't see the parallels between where you're at with your business and where you're at with Aaron."

In truth, she hadn't. So she just looked at her sister, blinking.

"Macie, you have planned and prepared for this business since you were in high school, getting every single duck exactly in a row. And you have planned and prepared to find the person you're meant to be with for the rest of your life since high school, getting every single duck there in a row too. And you have put time and energy and your whole heart into both of them. But when it comes down to making a really big commitment with either of them, you back away."

"I didn't back away— Aaron did!"

"And have you gone after him? Have you let him know how you feel, and that you think the relationship is worth fighting for? And what about before the breakup? That day when we were out Christmas shopping and you confessed that the two of you had been fake dating, you were backing away plenty. Were you backing away before then, too?"

Macie opened her mouth to respond, but nothing came out, so she closed it again. After a few moments, she looked down and said, "He said he doesn't want to get married. To anyone, ever."

"I know he did. Do you know if he still feels that way? Because the man I saw at the Christmas Kickoff party wore the face of someone who'd had a change of heart." Joselyn got up from the bed and walked to Macie's desk. "Where's your *Future Husband* list?"

"Middle drawer, right on top."

Joselyn brought the sheet of pale blue card stock filled with Macie's handwriting as a seventeen-year-old, written nearly a decade ago, and put it on the bed between them as she sat back down. The edges of the paper were a little bent and more rounded than they once were, after years of pulling the paper out and looking and re-reading it, making mental checkmarks with each guy she dated.

"Which of these attributes does Aaron fill?"

Macie went down the list, making a little checkmark with her finger with each item. Communicates with me well, is fun to be around, encourages me and supports me in my choices, takes care of me when I'm sick, will do crazy spontaneous things with me, knows how to cook, shows that he puts me before his friends, would make a good dad, and is kind to others.

"So basically all of them."

"My business looks good on paper too," Macie said, "but that doesn't tell the whole story. There have been times over the past few weeks when I've thought Aaron and I communicated super well, and on a level deeper than I've connected with anyone in a long time. Maybe ever. But then he ran into something that affected our relationship, and he didn't come to me with it.

"And since he didn't, we couldn't tackle it together and come up with a solution. He just let himself fall down a dark hole, and only came to me once he was resigned to living in that dark hole. How could we have a good partnership like that? I had thought he was a great communicator before this. See? There are just no guarantees. With Aaron or my business."

Joselyn reached out and held Macie's hands in hers. "You've planned and prepared well, Macie. You've built yourself an impressive safety net. There aren't guarantees that things will work out the way you planned. You know this better than most people do. When you make a huge big commitment and things go a different direction than you thought they would, you adjust, just like you've been doing all along without there being a big commitment."

Macie looked at the papers spread before her that, in black and white, showed the qualities of her business, and in blue and pencil lead, the qualities of Aaron, and whispered, "But I'm afraid." Her voice came out squeaky and small. She was afraid of making huge commitments to both of them and risking something going wrong. She was afraid of losing her business since so much of her heart was wrapped up in it. But most of all, she was afraid of losing Aaron, after having so much of her heart wrapped up in him.

"Do you know what the opposite of fear is?"

Macie looked up and met her sister's eyes, her head shaking a fraction.

"It's faith. Faith and fear can't co-exist, so if you choose one, the other disappears. I *know* it takes a big leap! It did for me, too. But you aren't going to get the truly great rewards if you choose fear over faith."

"Do you think I can take a leap of faith that big?"

"As your best friend, as a fellow businesswoman, and most importantly, as your sister, yes. I know you better than anyone, Macie. And without a doubt, *yes*."

twenty-two

AARON

Aaron knocked softly on the door and waited, shifting the big box that sat in his arms. A few moments later, Macie's mom carefully opened the door, a wide smile spread across her face, and whispered, "Hi, Aaron. Come in."

"Hello, Emeline. It's so good to see you again. Does anyone know?"

She shook her head. "Still just me and Joseph."

Aaron set the box down on the ground, took off his gloves and put them in his pockets, then handed his coat, scarf, and hat to Macie's mom.

"Macie is about to make an announcement," she said, still in whispered tones, "so I need to get back in there. But first," she led him to a small table under the big family picture that hung on the entry wall opposite the front door, "here it is." She handed Aaron a fancy box about the size of a shirt box, then reached out and placed her hand on Aaron's arm. She looked up at Aaron with a look of silent but complete approval on her face.

Aaron nodded down at the box in his hands and mouthed *Thank you for this*. Then Emeline turned and hurried around the corner into the family room that sat on the other side of the wall.

Muffled sounds and occasional laughter came from the other room. Aaron took a deep breath and crept near the opening so he could hear what was happening.

"Okay, enough with the balled-up wrapping paper war," Joseph said. "I believe Macie has an announcement she'd like to make."

"Grandpa!" one of Macie's older nephews said. "You can't throw one more after you called a cease-fire!"

"Oops. I better throw two more, then."

Judging by everyone's laughter and shouts, Macie must've intercepted the second one and tossed it right back at her dad. Then, except for the sounds the littlest kids were making and an occasional dog bark, everyone quieted down.

"Yesterday," Macie said, "Joselyn went all 'big sister' on me— but don't worry, not 'bossy big sister'"—

"Because she knows she'd have to fight me for that title," Nicole said, to lots of laughs.

"And she helped me to realize that I have been holding

back in a couple of areas of my life and that I was shying away from making long-term commitments because of some pretty deep-seated fears. She also told me that faith wipes out fear. Apparently, there were a lot of things I was unknowingly doing, and I can't say I wanted to believe that she was right about it."

"*Oof.*"

Based on the sounds and Marcus's burst of belly laughter, Aaron guessed that Joselyn had thrown a ball of wrapping paper at Macie.

He chuckled, knowing that by the sounds of things, Macie threw it right back.

When the noise died back down, Macie said, "So I did some pretty hefty soul-searching all day yesterday. And then last night when we were doing the live nativity and Riley, you were wearing your angel wings and halo, and Janet, you were dressed as Mary and had just found out that you were going to have baby Jesus, the angel said to Mary, 'Be not afraid.'

"And then Janet, you got this look of blissful contentment on your face, and I knew that's what I wanted. I wanted to not be afraid and to be willing to take two huge leaps of faith, even if it was over chasms so wide that I couldn't see the other side. Because with you guys cheering me on, how could I fail?"

Aaron could barely breathe as he waited to hear the rest of her announcement. A small scuffing sounded behind him, a shifting of position, and his attention went to the box still sitting near the door, wrapped in colorful Christmas paper.

"So last night, after everyone was all tucked into their sleeping bags all through the house, visions of sugarplums dancing in your heads, I took the first of two leaps. I logged on to Mom's and Dad's computer and signed the papers to buy Paws and Relax's building, and sent them off."

Cheers erupted from the room, and Aaron's heart swelled. Macie had done it. He knew how tough the decision had been for her to make, and he was so proud of her. It was obvious how much she cared about her business, and how much it meant to the people of Nestled Hollow, and he was thrilled she'd be able to keep it. He set the fancy box back on the table, and went over and picked up the box by the door.

The box was big enough to be rather awkward to carry, especially with its shifting weight. He turned the corner to the family room to see thirty-four people, all dressed in Christmas-colored pajamas and hugging and congratulating Macie, and all eyes flew to him.

"Aaron!" Macie said, a look of surprise on her face. But it looked like a happy surprise, which was much more than he expected after the way he had treated her. He breathed out relief. He had suspected that her second leap of faith involved him, but he wasn't sure if that leap was going to be away from him or toward him.

But either way, he was proud of her for making a tough decision, and he wanted to let her know that and show that he believed in her, even if it was coming a bit late. And then he'd need to convince her of how much he wanted that second leap of faith to be toward a future with him.

He didn't even have to say a word, and everyone found seats on the couches, chairs, and floor, leaving an open pathway between him and Macie. She stood in front of the crowd, wearing red, white, and green striped leggings, and a nightshirt with a Christmas tree printed on the front. In his jeans and button-down shirt, he suddenly felt very wrongly dressed for the occasion.

"I heard your announcement," he said, the smile spreading across his face. "I knew you could do it. I brought you something to show how much I believe in you." He lifted the box a bit and walked right up next to her.

Her eyes searched his face, and then she glanced at the box. Her face was full of questions, and he wanted to answer them, but first, he wanted her to open the box.

Her older brother Oliver got off his chair and moved it near Macie, so Aaron set the box down on top of it. But still, Macie's eyes wouldn't leave his.

"Open it already!" one of the kids called out.

Aaron wanted to give him a high five for saying what he was thinking, but he didn't want to take his eyes off Macie.

She lifted the tag on the top of the box and read out loud, "To my Mysterious Goddess, from your Dashing Man who believes in you one hundred percent." She smiled at him before lifting the lid off the top and then she gasped.

"Oh my goodness, you got me a dog!" She pulled the dog out of the box to the sounds of *Aww*'s and "he's so cute" from everyone in the room, and the dog immediately gave a happy bark. His coat was a milk-chocolate brown, and the reindeer antlers Aaron had put on the puppy right before coming into the house were still in place. The dog was still young enough that he had chunky toddler-like features, and his feet scrambled to find her as she pulled him to her, hugging him to her chest. He gave a second yip and licked her neck.

"From the shelter?" she asked.

"Of course," he said, and she looked at the dog like she loved him even more.

The dog was trying to climb her or get into a different position or just burn some energy after waiting so patiently, and she was struggling to keep hold of him and still be able to look at Aaron. He seemed to find a position he liked, though, and settled into her arms. "That was a huge risk, Aaron Hall! You knew I could only get a new dog if I bought my building. How did you know I would put in an offer?"

"You're an amazing woman, Macie. It's not hard to believe in you." She gave him a look that took his breath away and made him think that maybe he had a chance. He was suddenly very aware of how many people were in the room, and he cleared his throat. "He's just little now, but they said he'd likely be a medium-sized dog, and I figured that since you had big ones and smaller ones—"

"He's perfect. As perfect as could be. Does he have a name?" She rubbed a thumb behind his ears, and the dog leaned his head back, mouth open in obvious enjoyment.

Aaron reached out and petted the dog's head. "Nope. They found him wandering alone without a collar."

Macie looked the dog in the eyes, studying him. "A Christmas puppy— with antlers!— from my Dashing Man. Hmm. I think I'll name him Dasher."

As Macie looked at the puppy, her face bright and happy, Aaron knew, once again and with absolute certainty that what he wanted most in the world was to be able to wake up every morning for the rest of his life next to her. To face whatever challenges life threw at them, and to do it side-by-side with Macie, meeting those challenges together. "That's not the only thing I came here for."

"Oh?" Macie looked at him, her lips parted, an eyebrow raised. She set Dasher on the ground, and a few of her nieces and nephews gathered around him and petted him.

Aaron turned toward the door opening, but Macie's mom was already out of her seat and motioned that she would get the box. A moment later, she came back into the room and handed it to him.

The box shook slightly in his hands. For as sure and confident and at peace as he'd felt this morning, he had hoped that he'd be able to pull this off with a little more fearlessness. After having such a monumental change in heart and his entire way of thinking— something that only Macie could've affected in him— he was suddenly very worried that she didn't feel the same way.

And there were so many people in the room watching. It was a lot of people to make himself so vulnerable in front of. But it also felt exactly right to have them here.

Their relationship had begun under the guise of dating, and he'd be forever grateful for their pact because he'd have never gotten to know and love her without it. He'd realized that from the beginning, the parts of themselves that they'd been sharing and how they'd been connecting had been anything but fake. As he'd been drowning in his sorrows and looking back at the last several weeks with her, he knew he'd been connecting to the truest, most genuine, sincere, authentic person he'd ever met.

The thoughts calmed his nerves, the box stopped shaking, and his tight throat relaxed.

"Macie," he said, and all the chattering in the room hushed. "I met you at a time when I was most determined not to fall in love. I thought I was just getting out of the deal a teammate with a common goal— I didn't know I was partnering up with the one person in all the world with the power to shatter the stone around my heart.

"That day in the ice cream shop, I thought you were the most beautiful woman I had ever seen. Since then, I've found out that the beauty you have in here," he reached out and touched three fingers just above her heart, "far outshines it. You've introduced me to a kind of love that I didn't know existed, and I want to show you that same kind of love back. I want to be your teammate in life, Macie. Your partner in everything."

He took the lid off the top of the box and set it aside, revealing the stocking Macie's mom had made with his name on it, with two links already attached to it—one that he hoped Macie would want to link with hers, and one to link him to her family.

He got down on one knee to the collective sound of gasps from everyone in the room. "Macie Zimmerman, will you marry me?"

twenty-three

MACIE

Macie looked down at the stocking in the box, with her mom's signature beading and stitching, and with Aaron's name on it. Every year when her parents put up the linked stockings, she had imagined how it would look to have one up there with her future spouse's name on it. Seeing that stocking with Aaron's name on it felt exactly and completely *right*.

"You...You want to get married?"

Aaron chuckled. "I hadn't seen this coming, either. But apparently, all along it wasn't that I didn't want to get married— it was that I didn't want to get married to anyone who wasn't you."

She realized that she could deny it all she wanted, but Aaron was exactly what she'd imagined every day since the seventeen-year-old her had first made her *Future Husband* list. He had been her needle in the haystack all along, and deep down, she had known it even during the times when she'd allowed fear to try to convince her that she'd just been holding another piece of hay.

"So," he said, his voice coming out more unsure, "what do you say?"

"Oh, Aaron, yes! Yes! Of course, the answer is yes." She pulled him to his feet, wrapped her arms around his neck, and said, "Yes, I want to be your teammate in life, your partner in everything, your wife. I want to be the person you turn to, the shoulder you cry on, the one you laugh the hardest with, and the one you dream the biggest dreams with. You and me, hand in hand, facing everything life has in store for us, together."

Aaron set the box aside and wrapped his arms around her waist, holding her close. Their noses touched, and he said, "I've seen the way we are as partners, and I'm pretty sure there isn't anything we can't conquer."

She grinned and he grinned, and then she kissed that grin. His kiss back wasn't hesitant like the last time they'd kissed. It was soft and wonderful and full of confidence. Their lips moved together in perfect unison, like a dance that they'd practiced the steps to. She pulled him in closer. And then she realized that she was being kissed by her *fiancé*, and her kiss turned into a smile once again.

"Too much smoochie-smoochie!" her four-year-old

nephew Brighton said. "Everyone quick— cover your eyes!"

Macie burst out in laughter and Aaron's cheeks reddened.

"Oops," he said.

Macie just turned to face her family, then grabbed Aaron's hand and lifted it high, and then they both bowed, just like they'd done at the Winter Formal. She smiled at him to cheers and clapping. One room, and it was filled with all the people she loved more than anyone in the entire world.

After not seeing Aaron's face for several days, and fearing that she'd never see it regularly again, seeing him smile back at her brought her even more joy than she'd ever imagined she'd feel at this moment. "I love you, Aaron Hall. With my whole heart, with my whole soul, with my whole *everything*."

"And I love you, Macie Zimmerman. About a hundred times more strongly than I thought was even possible."

They stood there side by side, looking into each other's eyes, as happy chatter filled the room.

Macie's dad stood up and shook Aaron's hand, and said, "Welcome to the family, son. You're in our hearts for good now." Then he turned to the group and clapped his hands together. "I think there are two things that need to happen before we move on to the gingerbread house competition. Now I know you are just freshly engaged and don't even have a wedding date yet, but do either of you have any objections to linking Aaron's stocking right now?"

Macie saw the look on Aaron's face and thought that maybe, just maybe, having his stocking linked to everyone else's was just as important to him as it was to her. Her dad must've noticed, too, because he said, "I'll take that as not having any objections. What about the rest of you? Any objections?"

Marcus raised his hand. "I object to having more competition for Favorite Uncle."

Macie's dad laughed, and said, "I'll also take that as not having any objections. Emeline?" He held out his hand, and Macie's mom stood and put her hand in his. Then they turned and linked Aaron's stocking to Macie's, and then to the rest of the family. Her parents both turned back to face all of them, and Macie's dad said, "More than anything else, family matters. And we would like to officially welcome you to ours."

Aaron reached out like he was going to shake their hands and give them a heartfelt thank you; but instead, her parents enfolded him in a hug. And then Macie's brother Zach slammed into their group hug, wrapping his arms around them all. "Welcome to the family, bro."

"Stop hugging," six-year-old Sophie demanded, one hand on her hip and the other holding out a present.

"Grandpa, you said there were two things that needed to happen, and hugging wasn't one of them. *This* was."

Macie accepted the present and saw that the tag said it was to Aaron, and the *from* line was blank. When they'd opened presents earlier, she hadn't even noticed that there was one still unopened. Who had gotten a present for Aaron? She hadn't even guessed he would be there. But her mom motioned for her to give it to Aaron, so she did.

Aaron took off the wrapping paper, took the lid off the box, and started laughing. He pulled out a pair of Christmas pajamas. "I knew I was underdressed." He turned to her mom. "Thanks for having my back."

"Now hurry and change," Macie's brother Everett said. "I'm going for the 'tallest gingerbread house' award, and I need some better competition than these fumble-fingered troglodytes."

———

"I had fun today. Your family is very accepting." Aaron rubbed his hands down his pajama pants and then tapped his fingers on his knee.

"It's because they all have the Christmas spirit. Just wait until Valentine's Day—that's when the claws come out."

Aaron looked at her in alarm.

"Kidding! They love you." She watched as he jiggled the mouse connected to her laptop. They escaped the festivities not long after lunch and headed back to her place to wait for the video chat with his parents. "Why are you so nervous?"

"I'm pretty sure you've gathered that my family is not like yours."

"And you've never 'brought home' a girl before?"

"Not since Sabrina. And that was nine years ago." He looked up for a moment. "Looking back, that meeting didn't go very well. It's not too late to back out. Do you want to back out? I can tell Aliza to just let them know that I couldn't make it."

Macie put her hand on Aaron's leg. "Family is important. Whether it's big or small, functional or not so much, accepting or exclusive, they're important." She grabbed his hand with hers. "Side by side, together, we've got this."

Aaron looked at Macie, his gaze intent and searching and welcoming. He leaned forward and kissed her. His lips had barely touched hers when the incoming call alert sounded. Aaron took a deep breath, then said, "We've got this," and clicked to answer the video chat.

"Aaron! So good to see you. Merry Christmas!" His mom leaned closer to the camera, squinting. "Are those Christmas pajamas you're wearing?"

"Hi, Mom. Merry Christmas to you too."

"Seriously, son, it must be like two in the afternoon

where you are. Why on earth would you still be in pajamas? Remember when you used to dress nicely for our calls?"

"Mother, you're wearing a swimsuit."

"That's because I'm vacationing in Cabo San Lucas. Check out these white sand beaches." She turned her tablet around, giving them a view of the landscape.

"It looks beautiful there. And warm."

"Oh, it is. And I am here with a very good-looking and —Oh, it's your father." Aaron's dad's picture showed up on the screen. "Hello, Ken."

"Hello, Sheri." Aaron's dad's voice had been just as cold in his greeting to his mom as she had been in his. "Aaron! How are you doing, son? Wait, are those...Are those *Christmas pajamas* you're wearing?"

"Hi, everyone! Sorry I'm late," Aaron's sister Aliza said as her face popped up on the screen, and Aaron's grip on Macie's hand loosened just a bit.

"It's okay, honey," his mom said. "We already talked to you recently."

"Did I miss anything?"

"Just your brother showing up in pajamas," his dad said, and Macie quietly chuckled, just out of view of his family. Her laughing nearly made Aaron laugh out loud, so she put her hand over her mouth.

"So, no *announcements* or anything have been made yet?" Aliza asked.

"You already told us your announcement, honey."

"But it sounds like Aaron hasn't told you his."

Both of his parents looked into their cameras, their faces full of questions and impatience, while Aliza leaned back in her chair, arms folded, a smile spread across her face. Aaron looked at Macie and said, "Are you ready?" She nodded, and he turned the laptop so that the camera captured both of them in the frame. "Mom, Dad, Aliza, I'd like you to meet Macie Zimmerman. She's an amazing woman who, as of about five hours ago, is now my fiancée."

"Congratulations, son," his dad said. "Congratulations to both of you."

Aaron's mom's hand flew over her mouth. "You're getting married? Ken, our son is getting married!" She shouted loud enough that everyone on the beach probably heard, "My son is getting married! And so is my daughter!" She held the tablet out toward all her fellow beachgoers so they could see the evidence, but none of them seemed the least bit interested. She turned the tablet back to herself. "Oh my goodness, neither of my kids are going to die old and alone. Oh, I'm so happy!"

"Thanks, Mom," both Aaron and Aliza said at the same time.

"Oh, come on you two. You know you were both giving me plenty to worry about."

"Truthfully," his dad said, "I'm thrilled for both of you. I hope you're as happy as Felina and I are."

"And as happy as me and Carlos are," his mom quickly cut in, aiming the tablet toward a muscular, shirtless man in the lounge chair beside her.

Aaron looked at Macie, his face all love and smiles, and said, "I think we've got the happiness thing down."

AARON

With a blanket in his arms and Macie by his side holding two bowls of ice cream, Aaron made his way from the back door of Joselyn's house out across the grass, Reese, Lola, and Dasher joining them.

"It's still so muddy— I'm sinking!"

"Here, take this," Aaron said, holding out the blanket.

With both bowls of ice cream in her hands, Macie grabbed the blanket between her elbows, and then Aaron scooped her up into his arms, the blanket and bowls of ice cream now resting on top of her.

"Mmm," Macie said. "The last time you did this, it felt like an angel lifted me out of the land of the nearly dead and carried me to the land of salvation. It feels every bit as amazing even when I'm on top of the world."

He made a mental note to hold her in his arms like this

every chance he got. As he picked his way across the backyards that all came together in one, Macie snuggled in close enough that he could smell the scent of her shampoo —milk and honey from heaven—and he kissed her on top of her head.

Reese stayed right by their side, while Lola ran ahead to the picnic table she must've sensed they were headed to, and Dasher ran circles around them, yipping his excitement about being able to run around in grass that was turning green again.

When they reached the picnic table, he joined her and wrapped the blanket around both of their backs as they sat on the table, their feet on the bench. She passed him his *Maple, Please Bring Home the Bacon*, and picked up her *Is the Doctor Pepper In?*, and they each took a bite as the tractor rolled into place on the very last empty Zimmerman family lot, and started digging the hole for their future house.

"And the first scoop of dirt is out!" Macie said and held up her cup of ice cream.

Aaron bumped his bowl into hers and thought about their very first meeting over these same flavors. He had been so clueless back then about how much the trajectory of his life was about to change. What if he hadn't decided that the events of that day had called for ice cream, and he missed out on knowing how rich life could become?

"It's freezing out here!" Macie said as she scooted even

closer. "Whose crazy idea was it to celebrate this moment with ice cream anyway?"

Aaron laughed. "I believe that one was your crazy idea. It's one of the reasons why I love you."

"Right back atcha. I hear that marriages full of mutually crazy ideas make for the best ones." Macie grinned and then leaned in for a kiss.

Aaron pressed his lips against hers, their cold noses touching, the simple kiss sending a wave of warmth to his chest. Then, still less than an inch apart, he said, "We're going to have a house soon."

She smiled into his lips and said, "And we're going to be married soon," before kissing him again.

They both turned to watch as the tractor dug another scoop of dirt out of what would eventually be their basement. After going over so many plans, the weather had finally cooperated enough to start. Aaron took a bite of his ice cream. The past three months had been more blissful than he thought life could be. With as against marriage as he had been for so many years, he surprised himself by not having a single moment where he wondered if he had made the right choice or not. He just knew, without a doubt, that marrying Macie and starting a family with her was what was going to make him the happiest he could possibly be.

Feeling Macie's intense scrutiny of him, he turned to

face her again. "Uh oh. You've got your amateur Ice Cream Motivation Analyst face on."

Macie tapped her spoon against her lips. "I better analyze you then. Let's see. With that look, you must be...trying to decide what the chances are of you being able to finish your *Maple, Please Bring Home the Bacon* before Dasher jumps up here and eats it for you."

Aaron laughed as the puppy finally managed to jump onto the bench, bouncing and yipping. He pulled his bowl in closer to him. "That wasn't what I was thinking. Strike one for the amateur analyst."

She nodded. "Okay, you were thinking that I look great in this sweater you gave me for my birthday."

"While I have thought that *many* times today, it is not what I was thinking just now. Strike two. It's a good thing you didn't join the Ice Cream Motivation Analyst Guild. I don't think they'd be thrilled with your record right now." He took another bite of his ice cream.

"No, I'm going to get this. Just give me a minute." She studied his face, her own face so intensely serious that he had a hard time not either flinching or chuckling under the weight of it. "I've got it! You're thinking about how many children we should have."

His eyebrows shot up in surprise. "Impressive. The Guild is reviewing your application as we speak. They'll waive the application fee if you can also figure out how many I was thinking."

"Four."

She hadn't even paused to think about it first— her response was immediate. He hadn't come up with a number himself yet. "Why four?"

"Because that's how many it takes for a swim medley relay."

Aaron laughed so loud, he was positive that all her siblings heard it inside each of their houses. "Kids, you don't have a choice. You— you're the firstborn, so you must perfect backstroke, you've got breaststroke, butterfly for you, and I know you're the baby, but you need to bring some serious speed with your freestyle."

Macie grinned and took a bite of her ice cream.

"Unless, of course, you want a setup like this eventually." He motioned around to all of her siblings' houses. "Then we'll need seven kids."

"I don't know. I already promised Reese that he could have a houseful of puppies. And I sideways promised that Lola could too. I'm not sure how many we can fit in this house."

"Hmm. We're going to need more room." Aaron set his ice cream aside and stood up, letting his side of the blanket fall to the top of the picnic table. "I'll go tell him to dig a bigger hole."

Macie laughed and pulled him back down. "However many kids we end up having, I'm sure we'll find a way to fit."

He wrapped the blanket around them more tightly and pulled Macie in close. "As enjoyable as it is to be your fiancé, Macie Zimmerman, I am very ready to be your husband."

"Waiting stinks," Macie said. "It's like we're at the starting line to a wonderful life together, and we're just standing there. Waiting. It's right there, so close we can see it, and no one is *ever* going to sound the 'Go' horn."

"I would suggest that we elope, but I don't want to miss out on seeing what the Zimmerman family is like when you add aunts, uncles, cousins, and grandparents, from both sides to the mix." Truthfully, he couldn't even imagine how big that group would be.

"And if all those students of yours who were so determined to find you a wife by the end of the school year didn't get to come to the celebration, I think they might just plan a secret one for us, and then find some sneaky way to get us there."

Just picturing what they'd do made him chuckle. They were good kids. A little presumptive, but good. "So I guess we wait."

"Which comes with the added bonus of giving the contractor enough time to finish our house. Because otherwise, we'd be sleeping out here under the stars and cooking all our meals over that fire pit."

"As long as I get to be there with you, I wouldn't complain a bit."

"Who cares what temperature it is?" Macie said. "Baby, I'm never cold"—

Aaron laughed and finished the sentence, —"because you warm my heart."

Macie sighed and leaned her head on his shoulder, looking out at the tractor as it continued to dig the hole that, as they watched over the next few months, would slowly become their together home. "You know, I've imagined this moment so many times over the past...fifteen years, I guess— since I was thirteen and watched this same moment happen for my oldest brother and his fiancée. And in all my imagining, never did my brain come up with something this wonderful." She turned her face toward his. "You, Aaron Hall, are even more incredible than my very impressive imagination."

Then she turned toward him, put her hands on his cheeks, and pressed her lips against his. Lips that were soft, confident, and sure. He moved his hand up her back to rest at the nape of her neck, his fingers in her hair, and returned her kiss, his own lips filled with hope, possibilities, and excitement for their future together.

———

Author's note:

I hope you enjoyed reading Macie's and Aaron's story as much as I enjoyed writing it!

I hope you'll join me for Brooke's and Cole's story in the next Nestled Hollow book— *More than Friends in the Middle of Main Street*. I loved writing their story! They are such opposite characters, and it made for some really fun scenes. He's a single dad, too, which added another element that I had so much fun with.

Get More than Friends in the Middle of Main Street

Do you like audiobooks? I am putting more and more of my audiobooks on my YouTube channel every month. Subscribe so you'll be notified each time one releases.

May you have many hours of happy reading in your future!

—Meg

Read next:

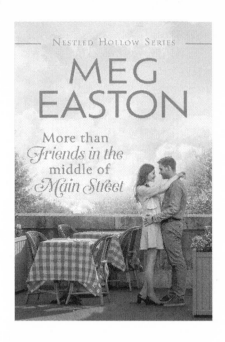

**One is spontaneous; the other is stable. One's
flighty; the other's down-home. He's a single
parent; she's determined to be single. What
happens when these best friends become more than
friends?**

Brooke McClellan is the owner of the shop Best Dressed
and knows how to do three things very well: design
amazing dresses, and stay far away from serious
relationships. She definitely doesn't date anyone from
Nestled Hollow, and especially not her best friend, Cole.

Whenever Cole Iverson isn't running his restaurant, Back
Porch Grill, he's taking care of his nine-year-old daughter

or tamping down the feelings he has for his best friend, Brooke. It's been three years since his wife died and he's ready to get remarried, but he knows it could never happen with Brooke.

When Brooke offers to help Cole plan the birthday party of his daughter's dreams, Brooke starts to realize that she has feelings for him. But are they opposites in too many ways for this to work? Are they willing to risk their friendship to pursue something more?

Pick up this sweet best friends romance

get the series

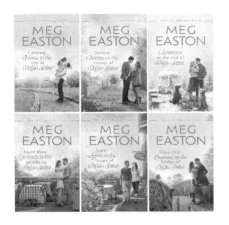

Coming Home to the Top of Main Street
Second Chance on the Corner of Main Street
Christmas at the End of Main Street
More than Friends in the Middle of Main Street
Love Again at the Heart of Main Street
More than Enemies on the Bridge of Main Street

about meg

Meg Easton is the *USA Today* bestselling author of contemporary romances and romantic comedies with fun, memorable, swoon-worthy characters, and settings you'll want to pack up and move to. She lives at the foot of a mountain with her name on it (or at least one letter of her name) in Utah. She loves gardening, bike riding, baking, swimming before the sun rises, and spending time with her husband and three kids.

She can be found online at www.megeaston.com, where you can sign up to receive her newsletter and stay up to date with new releases, get exclusive bonus content, and more.

If you liked this book please leave a review. Your review can help other readers find books they might fall in love with.

f facebook.com/MegEastonBooks

Made in the USA
Las Vegas, NV
10 February 2023

67258375R00148